The Great Convergence

A tale of strange encounters, even stranger goings on, scheming, chaos, greed, deceit, hilarity, triumph and just desserts!

Jess Miller

The Great Convergence

© 2000 Jester Publications & 2010 Jess Miller & MillerBooks   ISBN: 978-0-9565831-3-0

Jess's other titles:

How to Beat the Energy Thieves® And Make Your Life Better - Book 1
Alcohol, Drugs, Tobacco, Bullying, Stealing, Gambling, Gangs, Knives, Guns

© MillerBooks 2010   First published in 2010 by MillerBooks   ISBN: 978-0-9565831-0-9

If you don't understand that you have been created as energy then you can't determine how to protect the energy you are against everything in our world that will try to steal it from you in order to divert you from your true path and make your life hurt.
In this ground breaking self-help book Jess Miller gives clear, concise ways to deal with the energy thieves that are damaging your energy so you can forge your way down the road of good and guide yourself to a better life.

How to Beat the Energy Thieves® And Make Your Life Better - Book 2
Emotions, Food, People, Major Problems, Traumas, Winning.

© MillerBooks 2010   First published in 2010 by MillerBooks   ISBN: 978-0-9565831-1-6

How to stop emotions such as fear, loneliness, anger or hatred holding your energy hostage.
How to stop turning food into an energy thief.
How to get the better of people who are acting as energy thieves against you.
How to beat exam or public speaking nerves.
How to cope with financial wipe-out.
How to beat the energy thieves that live in your past and hurt you in the present.
Unique and powerful insights to help you protect your energy and find your way to a better life.

How to Beat the Energy Thieves® And Make Your Life Better - Book 3
Education, Indoctrination, The Media, Technology, Role Models, Gossip, Trivia, Self Importance and Arrogance

© MillerBooks 2010   **To be published in 2012** by MillerBooks   ISBN: 978-0-9565831-4-7

How your life teachers may not be teaching you the best way to live out your existence.
How your training by the system we live under enables it to control your energy.
How the media influences your opinions about life and the way you live it.
How technology can be a energy thief unless you use it only for what you absolutely need.
How role models can dramatically affect the direction of your life.
How idle gossip can ruin your life and the lives of others.
How the trivia of life can consistently bog down your energy.
How self importance and arrogance can steal away the energy that belongs to you.

We're All In This Together
Help Through Stressful and Depressive Times

© 2000 Jester Publications & 2010 MillerBooks   ISBN: 978-0-9565831-2-3

Explaining the journey we travel down into and back from depression and giving twelve simple, but powerful and proven self-help therapies that anyone can use to make themselves feel better in stressful or depressive times.

Acknowledgements and Thanks:

Research:

Duncan Gray, Chris Mansfield, Major Mike Morley, Frank Perry, Val Pitts, Michael Rovedo, Clive Sinclair, Harry Swanson, Helen Walford

Proof reading, critique, encouragement:

Gladys Miller, Betty Chadwick, Pat Madden, Rupert Suren

Special thanks to my good friend, the late author Douglas Sutherland, who told me that if I ever wanted to write a book the only way to succeed would be to write for four hours every day seven days a week and never miss a single day. That way I would not only start the book, but complete the task that defeats most people by finishing it.

Thanks forever Doug.

The Plan

Little Saddlington, England, 1979

The Crow that was a Rook tried to ease his way convincingly through the windy turbulence coming swirling up from the village.

As he flew across the square, constantly adjusting to each new burst of air, he was thinking to himself that it must surely be coming around to that dreadful nest building time again. It wasn't so bad everyone thinking of him as a lowly Crow, when in fact he belonged to a far nobler family, but the harsh reality of his life was having to live day in and day out with a really insufferable Old Crow.

'God I hate nest building' he thought to himself.

'She'll be at me all the time. Nag, nag, nag. Get this, fetch that.'

With his concentration momentarily lapsed a sudden powerful gust from around the side of the village hall caught him off guard, throwing him onto his back. Luckily he managed to dive out of the air current and, a blur of thrashing wings and tail feathers, proceeded to shoot with enormous velocity virtually vertically up the side of the building, just managing to clear the guttering that came far too close for comfort.

Straining to apply all the braking power he could muster he landed nearly perfectly on the apex of the roof and glanced anxiously around to see if any of his peers had noticed his avoidance of near disaster. Delighted to find that none of them had he began preening himself in an unconcerned manner as if he had deliberately intended to miss the building by those few inches and that, for him, this sort of aerobatic was an everyday occurrence.

Flying had been so much easier back at the Rookery with no buildings or alleyways to confuse and channel the winds and so, with the nasty prospect of this year's nest building looming, he began wishing he was back there.

Below him in the village hall Charles Montgomery was day dreaming about the love of his young life, Nancy Holroyd. At 20 years old he was so almightily smitten that to describe his case as hopeless would be an understatement for Charles loved Nancy more than oxygen.

She worked in a London advertising agency and they had met at a country house party near the village. She was 23, brunette with brown eyes that had welcomed him and a figure any man would notice. They had talked so effortlessly that soon both had been lost deep in conversation, oblivious even to their hosts. After that it had been phone calls and letters and rushed meetings, if Charles was ever able to get a day off work to take the train to London.

Getting a day off from Rubicon & Shipley, the village auction house where he worked, was almost impossible. His tyrannical boss, Eric Shipley, was an awkward, bombastic man who made Charles' life absolute hell by constantly pushing too much work on him and then haranguing the young man for not having completed it on time. Paying him but a pittance Shipley was forever

1

trying to catch Charles out making personal phone calls at the firm's expense and, if successful, would dock his pay by some ridiculous amount. His manner was domineering, sneering and belittling and he would regularly rant and rave at Charles in front of the secretary.

Originally supposed to work five days a week, Charles had been unable to stop Shipley raising this to six days for the same pay and then throwing a few Sundays into the equation, but for only a paltry one and a half times the pay rate.

It had not taken long for Charles to come to hate Eric Shipley.

'I hate Shipley and I love Nancy. I love Nancy and I hate Shipley', he mused to himself.

"Montgomery!"

"Yes, Mr.Shipley?"

"What are you doing, boy? Have you finished arranging the advertising for the next sale?"

"Yes, yes I have Mr.Shipley. All the adverts are in, but I couldn't get us into the Chronicle. We were too late for the deadline, sir."

"Typical! If you would get on with your work instead of day dreaming we'd have that advertisement running. As it is we're going to lose business through your complete inefficiency. Why I bother to employ you and have to suffer your stupidity losing me money I do not know. If you don't buck your ideas up you'll be facing the sack, do you understand, boy?"

"Yes, Mr. Shipley."

"You better get on preparing for the next auction and this time reserve the advertising space first and then start work on the catalogue and I don't want to see any mistakes in this one. I'm fed up with having to explain them to people at every sale so just you make sure you proof read the catalogue properly for once. I intend taking in almost five hundred lots of house contents, farm equipment, livestock and antiques, so this will be our biggest ever sale and just you make sure you get everything right. I want the most comprehensive advertising we've ever had and if this one fails you're fired! Got it?"

"Yes, Mr.Shipley. Yes, sir. Got it."

"Well, get on with it then. I'm going out to lunch with Mr.Rawlston."

With that he left, slamming the front door leaving Charles and the secretary looking at each other. The secretary felt sorry for Charles, knowing the mammoth amount of work he faced. She had always helped him but this time there would have to be unpaid overtime for weeks to get it all done. Charles thought about the prospect for at least a whole minute and then rang Nancy at work. She guessed from the hesitancy in his voice that something was wrong.

"Don't tell me you aren't coming to London on Sunday, please Charles."

"I can't Nancy, Shipley's given me a huge sale to organise."

"Why on earth do you bother staying with that obnoxious man! He's always giving you too much work and it's not fair on either of us! I just never get to see you Charles."

"I know, but what can I do?"

"We must be able to do something about it, couldn't he employ someone to work with you?"

"I doubt it, he's the meanest sod on the planet. He treats everyone so appallingly, no one around here has a good word to say about him."

"Why don't the villagers just boycott his auctions or throw him out or do something?"

"Apathy I guess, they're all good country folk and I don't think they would have it in them to go through with anything like that even though they'd like to see the back of him."

"Maybe the two of us should get rid of him."

"Us? How? Whatever could we do? There's no way to get Shipley out and no way to get him to behave reasonably either, anyway I need this job."

"What we really need is a plan."

"A plan? What kind of a plan? All I do is organise the advertising and the catalogues and that's a standard job in an auction house. Then there's the secretary, the removals people and Shipley and that's about it."

"I wonder what would happen if I took charge of placing the auction advertising and I made sure the biggest amount of people he's ever seen turn up at his auction? Would he be able to cope?"

"Probably not, he's not too good on organisation and he's a bit slow as an auctioneer."

"Mind you, we could make sure he gets stuck with a huge advertising bill afterwards."

"What? But I'll get the sack! What would I do, Nancy? I don't have any qualifications."

"Well, we'll just have to find you something in London, won't we? I'm sure one of my friends will give you a job. Then we would be able to see each other all the time. After all, if I can't get to see you, why am I going out with you?"

She had touched a raw nerve, the risk of losing her was far too great for Charles to contemplate. Even so trying to mess up Shipley's auction would be a daunting step for a young man to take.

"But where would I live? I don't have any money and you're the only person I know in London."

Nancy was not going to be deterred.

"Actually I was thinking of renting a bigger apartment. One with two bedrooms this time and you could have the second bedroom if you contribute to the rent. Then we could be together."

"Oh, I don't know, Nancy, I mean what if I didn't get a job? What if you didn't find an apartment? What if Shipley comes after me for going over our advertising budget?"

"Charles Montgomery, get a hold of yourself! We will simply have to have everything properly planned and worked out. You could be organising this one last auction whilst I get us a flat and then you could leave your job and move straight in. It will be alright, you'll see, I mean we can't guarantee everything in life, but at least we would be together and that's a lot better than the way Shipley's forcing us to be right now, isn't it?"

She was absolutely determined to solve their problems and was not going to give up easily, for Nancy loved Charles as much as he loved her. As they talked their plan took shape and Charles found himself becoming bolder as they got deeper and deeper into the plot to teach Shipley a lesson he wouldn't forget.

Once he could see that the auction would be bombarded with people and Shipley would be rubbing his hands about all the money he would be going to make, only to find later that the advertising costs would most probably take it all away, Charles began throwing in some of his own ideas. He felt he should get the printer to include some expensive colour photographs in the auction catalogue, perhaps a separate colour insert sheet that could hopefully be kept out of Shipley's sight until it was too late for him to do anything about it. Also he should quit his job immediately after the auction and vanish well before his boss could get at him.

Shipley would then be left facing all of the after sales work involving getting all the purchasers' money in, returning any unsold lots to their owners, delivering uncollected lots to their respective buyers and distributing their portion of the auction proceeds to the respective vendors. Charles certainly knew how much work that normally was, but this time the workload would be far greater if he and Nancy could somehow create a really huge auction. Shipley would have no option but to part with all the money he had taken in to his vendors as he was under legal obligation in his terms and conditions of business to pay out to each sale's vendors within seven days. This was a condition he had originally self-imposed to encourage people to sell things through his auctions and get paid quickly. Finally there would be the costs of the advertising, the printing of hundreds of extra catalogues and the colour inserts to pay for.

Charles became enthralled with the idea of the plan as he began to see a way to get back at Shipley and be released from what was currently not a very enjoyable existence. He became enthralled too at the thought of eventually being with Nancy, but he did wonder how long this two bedroom business she was on about would have to last.

A few days later Nancy was having lunch with International News Service director Neil Darnley.

"Now then, Neil, I want you to do something for me."

"Would it have anything to do with sex?" he asked, smiling broadly.

"No, it certainly would not and you're a married man, remember?"

"Oh yes, sorry, completely slipped my mind. So what do you want today lovely Nancy?"

"I want you to put something out on the wire, something I need advertising."

"Advertising? Isn't that your job? We dispense news not advertising my dear."

"Exactly. This is both news and advertising and I need it dispensing. Now I know you can do it so please don't make out that you can't. Here is all the detail you need, I just want your word that you'll put this together for me."

Neil looked at the papers.

"An auction? You want me to publicise an auction in somewhere called Little Saddlington? I've never heard of the place. Don't be ridiculous Nancy, I really can't do this, after all I could lose my job. What on earth do you think you're doing?"

"Listen to me very carefully, Neil. I am buying you lunch am I not?"

"Yes."

"And you would like to do me a favour, would you not?"

"Of course."

"And we are both going to keep quiet about each other's secrets, are we not?"

"Oh, absolutely. What do you mean? I don't know any of your secrets."

"No, but I know some of yours Mr.Darnley, don't I?"

"Do you? ...Oh, yes...Oh, dear me... I'd quite forgotten."

His look was one of distinctly unhappy remembrance of some past dreadful indiscretion.

"But you wouldn't Nancy, I mean you wouldn't really, would you?"

She looked at him impassively, determined to get what she wanted for Charles.

"Now then Neil, how extensively are you going to cover my auction? After all it does have an unlimited budget."

She stared deeper into his eyes while flashing him a disarming smile as he tried to chew his lunch with increasing difficulty.

"Well I really don't know. I mean are we talking editorial?"

"Definitely."

He sighed and raised his eyebrows enquiringly.

"Big coverage?"

Her look was dismissive.

"Huge coverage?"

Nancy slowly shook her head. Neil Darnley was now a most unhappy man.

"Oh, alright then, enormous coverage, worldwide stuff, I can't do more than that as you well know."

Nancy smiled at him, the die had been cast

Little Saddlington

Herpes was a decidedly odd looking dog.

He was like a not fully mixed mixture as if various bits from various dogs had been stuck to each other in some great hurry. Forever getting into fights he would often appear covered in mud and muck, his grey coat with clumps of hair missing and his face and legs covered with cuts and sores.

He also had a famous almost legendary achievement to his name which was that from time to time, due to his rough and varied diet based on eating anything he could find, whether edible or not, Herpes could break wind with such a dreadful result that he could just about clear the local pub.

His owner, Bob, was a tramp-like figure who did odd jobs about the village and claimed social security. He always wore an old raincoat tied around the middle with a piece of string as tramp-like people do and, with his dishevelled appearance and swarthy features, he appeared somewhat ferocious looking although no one actually knew whether he was or not. Bob and Herpes, who was known to the villagers as the 'Erp, certainly complemented each other and appeared just as though they were part of some dangerous band of brigands.

People would move along the bar whenever they entered the Flying Start, the local pub, but no one ever told Herpes to leave as none of them were quite sure about what Bob might do and nobody really wanted to find out. So they put up with his dog's occasional use of reverse aromatherapy and somewhat stupidly would feed the 'Erp on crisps, bits of sandwiches, leftovers and all the things that unfortunately increased the likelihood of the very gas explosion they all so intensely disliked.

Dirk and Terry were poachers.

Like Bob they were on government handouts and poaching was a useful supplement to their meagre income. Rabbits, pigeons, deer, pheasants or salmon, if it was out there they would have a go at it. Unfortunately they had recently been caught one too many times and consequently both now had form, having just spent four weeks at Her Majesty's nearest hotel. This was the result of a disastrous early morning's poaching expedition on Rawlston Manor Estate, where they had been apprehended by the gamekeeper. The estate owner, Mr.Rawlston, had preferred charges against them despite the local policeman having assured him that a warning would suffice.

The police sergeant, Bert Hughes, knew Dirk and Terry well, knew where they operated and could basically nail them both whenever he wanted. This he would only ever do if someone complained about them as he would occasionally find a brace of pheasants or rabbits hanging on the back door handle of his house and he loved a bit of pheasant and rabbit too for that matter. As long as they kept their heads down and didn't do too much harm in the district he turned a blind eye most of the time. After all they were not really serious villains. He found that having a severe word with them was usually enough to encourage a curtailment of their activities for a couple of weeks and he had been somewhat annoyed at their having been prosecuted this last time.

Not only would the two rabbits and one pheasant they had been caught with not have bankrupted the estate, but in the past they had forewarned him on a couple of occasions when serious gangs of poachers had visited the district, resulting in his having made more that one notable arrest. It had been a sensible, unwritten agreement, but now, to his loss, they had totally clammed up.

There had been great anger in the village at the loss of their village hall.

No longer could the villagers enjoy their coffee mornings, bingo, raffles, bridge evenings and the occasional travelling act. Shipley had somehow bought it from right under their noses and in it he had opened his new business, Rubicon & Shipley. The main office of the business, housing Charles and the secretary, was next to the front door. Shipley's own office was out of sight at the back, around behind the stage that ran across the far end of the hall. The stage had made a perfect situation for an auctioneer as he could run each auction from a kind of pulpit positioned to one side of it next to the large disused fireplace. Items to be auctioned were laid out on tables on the stage with each being held up for the people in the hall to see before being sold. They were then carried off to one side whilst those items still to be auctioned were entered from a storeroom halfway along the passage to Shipley's office. Rows of seating ranged back from the stage almost to the front door of the hall with a space down either side for people to gain access. The capacity was supposed to be three hundred people, but they had never approached even half that number at their busiest auction. Outside Shipley had put up open pens for farm livestock down one side of the building, allowing him to go to the window that overlooked them to sell the animals.

The front of the hall led out onto the square that had buildings on three sides and the fourth, opposite the hall, opened out onto the village green. Beyond the buildings to one side of the square was the main road through the village, which was joined by a minor road behind the square on the opposite side to the green. A short way along the main road was the Flying Start, which backed onto the green and past the Flying Start came the river, forming a natural border around the far side of the green, flowing under the bridge and down the other side of the main road from the pub as it followed its winding course along the valley. The river brought life to the sleepy village in the form of ducks, swans and the occasional kingfisher or leaping salmon. A huge raft of ducks would sometimes leave the river and waddle their way to the square to gorge themselves on their private food supply, kindly provided by the villagers, before nestling down for an after dinner nap on the green. The square had once been host to a thriving Sunday market, but now it was overgrown with mosses clinging to the base of the old buildings and weeds and grasses sprouting from around its ancient paving stones.

Charles had thrown himself into his work with a determination the secretary had not seen before and he didn't seem to be daydreaming so much anymore. Occasionally his girlfriend would telephone him and he would talk to her in hushed tones, but afterwards he would get straight back to the job in hand and he certainly was eating up the mountain of work they had to complete. Shipley's descriptions of the items to be auctioned, dictated onto tape, were transcribed by the secretary and Charles co-ordinated the labelling of each of the lots as they came in and tied up the paperwork with the respective vendors. The stage and the back room they used for storing the auction items were rapidly filling when Shipley announced he had negotiated the sale of the contents of a large farm in the next valley, where the tenant had passed away and the family wanted everything sold.

"But Mr.Shipley, where are we going to store everything? We're almost full now and I'm nearly at your five hundred lot figure with quite a way to go."

"You don't need to worry about that Montgomery because I'm making arrangements to hire a large marquee to display the remaining sale items in. We're going to erect it on the village green. I've decided to make this a really stupendous auction by holding it over two days and just you make sure that it is stupendous or you will be leaving us, remember?"

"Yes, Mr.Shipley, I'll make sure it's a stupendous auction alright."

Charles thought to himself that it might turn out to be slightly more than stupendous the way enquiries were already coming in. The secretary had asked him why they were suddenly getting requests for catalogues from abroad, which they had never had before. Charles had done his best to convince her that it was probably just a freak of the business. Unconvinced she had told him that enquiries for catalogues were already approaching the two hundred mark and again asked for some explanation as she was concerned about the cost of posting them overseas.

Charles had tried to reassure her.

"Look, this is going to be a very busy auction. Mr.Shipley wants it to be a success and I'm working as hard as I can to make sure that it will be. We've got some very exciting stuff to sell and I'm really glad all these enquiries are coming in, aren't you?"

But the secretary wasn't totally sure that she was.

The Major

"Margaret!"

Major George Roberts awoke rising upright in his bed shouting his wife's name. Sweat poured from him as he shook from the memory of the nightmare and the sudden damning realisation that his wife of thirty two years was no longer with him. He stared into the darkness as he sat shivering and shaking from the noise of the explosions, the smell of the cordite, the burning and the screams of the men dying around him still so vividly and terrifyingly with him as it had been since that fateful day.

In March 1941 a twenty five year old squadron tank commander was retreating along with the rest of the British Eighth Army from Rommel's first great push across the North African desert. Only a short time before the retreat George Roberts had been involved in the attack on the Italian 10th army, driving them from Egypt through Libya to their final defeat at El Agheila in two short months. Now the roles were reversed as Rommel began to push the British back towards Tobruk. In the headlong rush to get away from the German advance logistics became badly disrupted, leaving them unsupplied and unsupported. They were so low on fuel he was forced to order a halt at a place called Wadi-el-Jabrin and either make a stand or surrender.

He decided to make a fight of it as his men knew he would.

He had hoped they would get lucky and would not be facing the heaviest part of the German attack or maybe, God willing, it would pass them by altogether. As the sands of time ran out he radioed squadron headquarters to find out about fuel, food and medical possibilities.

There were none.

Left without options he radioed battalion headquarters and announced his desperate plan. Through the crackling reception he thought he made out something about their stand possibly buying the retreating forces some time then further detail of the desperate logistics position became lost as the transmission broke up.

And so ten Matilda and four Cruiser tanks, stragglers that had joined them during the retreat, hunkered down in the dunes to await the inevitable artillery barrage and oncoming German Panzers. Neither the Matilda nor the Cruiser with their two pounder main guns and 7.62mm. machine guns were much of a challenge for the Panzer. In the freezing cold desert darkness they waited. The tank crews and the remnants of the infantry they had managed to carry with them from the conflict moving from tank to tank trying to boost each other's morale. Some, although never using the actual words, to wish good luck to their mates and indicate goodbye. Many sat quietly meditating in their tanks knowing full well what must be coming now that the German advance was right on top of them. Others enjoyed a last cigarette, all of them knowing they were but a final, futile defiance in the face of hopeless odds.

The young Major tried to lift the pressure on his own tank crew by talking to them about his life's passion for salmon fishing. He had told them of it before and found that it helped them relax as he conjured up pictures of the great rivers and valleys, the hills and green fields of England. But even as he spoke there were flashes on the horizon and countless artillery shells were incoming. The noise of the explosions was deafening, the tanks swaying from the blasts. Sand, dust and smoke filled the air and then the Panzers opened up. One by one the British tanks were hit with many exploding into searing fireballs, their crews screaming, roasting, dying.

Having taken a direct hit themselves the Major, now wounded in the shoulder and leg, gave the order to abandon the tank. Upon hitting the ground he saw the full carnage, the rout unleashed upon his men, machine gunned and slaughtered as they tried to surrender with him standing there powerless to help. Then a mortar round blew him off his feet unconscious. That was all he would remember for the next month and when he came out of coma he was in a German field hospital near Benghazi from where he was shipped to Italy as a prisoner of war. He would never be able to come to terms with the fact that those who had so nearly killed him and slaughtered his men had saved his life, nor that his final stand at Wadi-el-Jabrin had been the most terrible defeat.

Unceasingly and remorselessly down the years the nightmares had tormented him, driving his relentless cross examination of the decisions he had made back then ever onwards. Night after night he relived the horror, unable to free himself from the responsibility, the guilt and the memories of the dead.

Now, at sixty three years old, this constant mental oppression had taken its physical toll. His memory was failing, his speech becoming hesitant and he had become gaunt, almost haggard. Ever the military man he still walked erect, but increasingly he swayed to the side of his old leg wound and sometimes he became light headed and would have to sit and wait until the spell of dizziness passed.

With his wife gone he had slipped into the way of barely looking after himself, his clothes had become tatty, his appearance unkempt and some days he forgot to shave. Running out of money he was barely able to afford the rent on the cottage and the stretch of river he had been leasing from Rawlston Manor Estate for twenty five years. Twenty five years of fishing 'his own' stretch of water, watching the passing runs of salmon from his window, enjoying the fish he caught and even those he lost and enjoying the different seasons and happy days with Margaret. God had seen fit to take his good wife with the cancer one year before. He had nursed her day and night until the end, able only to watch helplessly as she withered and finally died. She was buried in the local cemetery and he visited her grave most days, making sure it was pristine in every way and placing the wild flowers she had so loved there whenever he could find them.

Slowly he got off the bed, put on his dressing gown and slippers and went downstairs to make tea. It was 4.30a.m. Only the perception of first light was in the sky as the river slid past, silent and dark. He busied himself amongst his fishing tackle, wiping traces of sweat from his face with the tea cloth. Maybe he should tie a salmon fly? A therapy he knew would settle him. The kettle boiled and he made his tea, a frail and lonely old tank commander brewing up in the dark. He sipped the tea and opened the front door of the cottage. As he stood in the doorway, filling his lungs with the fresh early morning air he could just make out the darkened river. Feeling at one with nature as he always had he made the same decision he always had. He would take his fly rod down to the Railway Pool and wait for the light to see if there was a fresh run salmon lying there.

His own revitalising remedy.

Geoffrey Rawlston of Rawlston Manor Estate, a short, pot-bellied, seedy little man with a round face and pallid complexion was landlord to the Major's cottage and fishing. The owner of the Manor for the last twelve years he had renamed the estate after himself upon purchasing it. The estate comprised a sizeable farm, some woods that provided good pheasant shooting, a two mile stretch of river, which the Major's three quarters of a mile split in two, and the manor itself, a large Edwardian house situated in a beautiful hillside location overlooking fields that swept down to the river and the village of Little Saddlington.

From the moment he had arrived Rawlston's chief desire had been to get the cottage and the piece of river that the Major leased back into his own hands. His scheme would then be to rent out the cottage with two miles of fishing by the week at extortionate rates that would bring in almost six times what the Major was paying. Once a proper fishing clientele and a track record of catches was established he would be able to timeshare the fishing and make himself a stack of money. Rawlston had done everything possible at every opportunity to try and get the Major out. He had raised the rent at each three yearly review by the maximum allowed under the terms of the lease with any negotiation being rudely dismissed. He had insisted on the Major paying for the renewal of guttering, down pipes, broken roof slates and the regular painting of window frames, doors and the exterior of the cottage all in the hope that financial collapse would force him to vacate, but to no avail. The Major had somehow managed to keep going and enjoy the remainder of his twenty five year lease right up to this, its final year. But now his money was almost gone and soon his cottage and beloved fishing would be as well.

Nobody in the village had a good word to say about Rawlston.

He was an arrogant, pompous man who ignored them most of the time and bulldozed straight through anyone who got in his way to get what he wanted. He had financially backed Shipley's new auction business as a silent partner, engineering their buying the village hall without anyone knowing it was for sale. He had achieved planning permission for a small housing development on the edge of his estate, on land zoned for agriculture, by bribing the local planning officer and had utilised the same method to gain a reduction in the rates that the estate paid to the local council. Although he had wealth he had demonstrated his Scrooge like qualities time and again. His staff were lowly paid as were his estate workers and the beaters at his pheasant shoots. No one knew or could find out where he or his money had come from and, as he was in consequence a mystery, stories about him abounded. His one weakness was that occasionally he would drink too much and turn into a romantic drunk, capable of singing songs and reciting poetry so badly and with such mock emotion that he would make a complete spectacle of himself, much to the amusement of the patrons of the Flying Start who had suffered these pathetic performances on more than one occasion.

Rawlston had taken every opportunity to be rude to George Roberts, mocking him in front of the villagers and forever making derisory remarks about 'Monty's Major'. He represented everything the Major disliked, a self important, arrogant bully with money. Being constantly talked down to over the years had made the Major's blood boil, but no matter how distasteful it was for him to have to deal with Rawlston he had been summoned to a meeting at the estate office and had no option but to go.

"I suppose you've had time to read your lease over the last twenty five years and that you know it's renewable?" sneered Rawlston as he sat with his smug looking lawyer looking across the desk at the Major.

"At my discretion, of course, but according to the lease I 'cannot unreasonably withhold my permission'."

He looked to his lawyer who affirmed the point.

"However, I have the right to place a premium on any new lease that I grant. You agree that this is correct and that I am acting fully within my rights?"

"Yes."

"Good! Then I am fixing the level of premium for a new twenty five year lease at twenty five thousand pounds! So if you do not pay me that sum by the time your lease expires at the end of June you can vacate my cottage and my fishings! Do you understand? Here it is in writing. Going to give us any arguments are you?"

Of course George Roberts understood. Completely boxed in he also saw little point in engaging in conversation with Rawlston, who knew full well that never in a million years would he be able to afford two thousand pounds for a new lease let alone the preposterous amount of twenty five thousand. So as the two of them awaited his reaction he simply picked up the piece of paper, got unsteadily to his feet, looked straight back at them without showing the slightest emotion and silently left the office. He walked slowly down the hill and crossed the fields that swept gently down to the river and the village. As he opened the side gate to the churchyard he was feeling the need to speak with Margaret.

"Well old girl it looks like I've had it this time. There was just a glimmer of a way out as we knew, but now it's been closed. Anyway there's no way I could really have afforded to stay here, the money's nearly gone and soon the cottage and the fishing will be as well. Perhaps it's better you're not here to have to go through all this. I don't really know where I'll be going and I don't quite know how I'll survive. Must be some sort of a home for people like me. Yes, that's it, a home. I suppose my pension might cover it, it certainly doesn't cover the rent any longer."

He sighed and his shoulders sagged.

"You know, I don't really feel there's much point in carrying on anymore."

After some time lost in his thoughts he smiled down at her grave.

"We did have it good though, didn't we? I'm so grateful for the years we enjoyed together, you saved me from going completely mad, you know. I love you Margaret and I miss you and I always will."

He turned away and walked slowly back to the cottage. Once there he sat in his den amongst his fishing things and looked around the walls at the photographs of himself and Margaret on their wedding day, photographs of him fishing the river and photographs of the two of them with their only son, their son who was no more.

The car crash that had taken him, at the tender age of eighteen, had claimed the lives of three of his young friends as well. Neither the Major nor his wife had been able to get over their loss. With his son and his wife gone he was alone in the world and soon he would be homeless and penniless. He looked over at the old brassbound chest, knowing full well its contents. He gazed at the chest for a long, long time. Finally he poured himself a large, straight whisky and began to drink it. Outside the breeze gently murmured through the trees as the light failed and a screech owl cried, heralding yet another lonely night, another night to be filled by the relentless nightmares, another night to be torn apart by the awful recurring memories of the past, another night to be faced alone.

He opened the drawer of his desk and there lay the brass key.

Turning it in the lock he lifted the lid of the chest and rummaged about inside. Finding what he had been after he returned slowly to his desk carrying his service revolver. He sat there motionless for sometime as if studying it, then he took a long, steady drink of whisky, emptied the glass, poured himself another and began to undo his tie.

That evening Rawlston simply could not resist celebrating his having defeated the Major and the fact that at long last he would be gaining vacant possession of his cottage and fishing. In the Flying Start he was buying drinks for everyone, recounting tales of estates he had owned, people he knew and namedropping and puffing himself up with even more importance than usual. The locals were surprised to find this normally selfish man buying them round after round of drinks. Bob and Herpes ignored him, well the 'Erp always ignored everyone, although Bob still took the drinks that Rawlston offered throughout the evening. The pub filled up, the ale flowed and talk and laughter filled the air as tongues loosened.

Outside the evening river mist was moving in and before long Dirk and Terry slipped unnoticed from the bar, for they did have one place to go poaching that the policeman did not know about. A short distance upstream from the pub was the bridge and they had devised a method of clambering down and each standing on one of the flat foundations that supported the arch, which they could do as long as the river was not running too high. Facing each other across the span under the bridge one would throw a rope across to the other with which a net was promptly hauled across. The net was weighted at the bottom and salmon swimming into it were caught by the gills to be dragged out and taken all of fifty yards and sold to Mickey, the landlord of the Flying Start. It was simple and it worked and nobody knew, except for Dirk and Terry and Mickey and Mrs. Mickey. Mickey paid them cash which they spent in the bar, which suited him fine as business was never that good in such a small community.

Soon the two of them were in position under the bridge with the net set and held tight between them as the current pushed it about.

All they had to do now was wait.

Before long Rawlston had become hopelessly drunk and to their relief had finished regaling the locals with his boring stories and poetry. He left the pub and weaved his way towards his car. As he looked across the river through the mist and his haze of inebriation he was just able to make out a cluster of bushes on the far bank. Mistaking their dark outlines for a gathering of people his brain went into romantic overdrive.

Were these not his faithful troops, massed and awaiting his command?

His knights of old ready to do his bidding?

He stumbled his way to the bridge where it took him several attempts to climb up onto the parapet and, once there, even more attempts to get unsteadily to his feet. Swaying about he tried to focus on the bushes as they kept coming and going in the swirling mist. Surely he was meant to lead these valiant men into battle? Completely overtaken by drunken melancholy he began reciting Henry the Fifth's great speech.

"Once more unto the breach, dear friends, once more!" he shouted out in the general direction of his 'men', flailing his arms about as he attempted to keep his balance.

Below him the two poachers had been waiting patiently and it had seemed as though salmon were not running that night, but just as they were about to give up and go home something big and powerful suddenly breached the net. Caught by the gills the mighty salmon thrashed in the stream threatening to pull them both in. It was a real brute of a fish and they could barely hold their own against it. As they struggled to get the better of it they could hear the noise of Rawlston's drunken oratory from above.

"What the bloody hell is that?" shouted Terry.

"God knows, just get the bloody fish in!"

"Get it in yourself, I'm nearly off the bridge!"

Rawlston, now swaying about like a tree in a tempest, had been unable to remember most of the words to the speech and had rapidly reached the final crescendo of his attempt to rouse his 'men' to battle. Waving his troops forward he shouted out at the top of his voice, "...and upon this charge cry God for Harry, England and Saint George!"

For a moment or two, as he lost his balance, it seemed as if he was going to fall backwards onto the road over the bridge. However his gyrations managed to save him from the injuries such a fall might have inflicted. Instead he launched himself the opposite way, out into space from the parapet, hitting the water like an exploding depth charge a split second later right on top of the two struggling poachers. As the current pushed him into the net his weight added to that of the fish and pulled the two of them straight off the bridge into the river alongside him. Together the three of them, tangled up in the net along with the huge salmon, were carried splashing, cursing and crying for help down the river past the Flying Start where, due to the noise of the revelry inside, no one could hear anything of their plight.

Dirk and Terry had no option but to save Rawlston's life. The thought of not doing so did indeed cross their minds, but despite their hatred of the man who had put them in prison they were poachers, not murderers. Eventually and in spite of all their struggling and floundering about they somehow managed to make it to the side of the river. Pulling the drunken, waterlogged and semi-conscious Rawlston up onto the bank they hurriedly retrieved the net, only to discover there was a large hole in it and that the mighty fish had escaped. They looked at each other mouthing obscenities, bundled the net up and melted into the night.

At well past midnight the sodden and intoxicated Rawlston burst into the Major's cottage.

Throwing the door open he lurched inside, staggering into the main room as the Major, now dressed in full military uniform, appeared from his den. Rawlston stumbled, fell over a table, then got uncertainly back to his feet.

"Got the money have you, you silly old bugger? Hah-hah!"

"You're drunk you miserable man! Get out of my house!"

"What are you all dressed up like a Christmas turkey for? Monty coming to dinner is he? Or are you getting married?"

"I'm warning you, Rawlston! Get out of my house or you'll regret it!"

"Nyaaah! Piss of you stupid old Corporal! I'm not afraid of you and I've got you now, haven't I? You see all this? It's all bloody finished! You've got no money! Can hardly pay your rent, never mind buy yourself a new lease! This is the end of Monty's Major and good riddance to you, you old bastard!"

Such was the anger inside the Major his look bordered insanity.

In his hand he held the revolver.

"It's about time the world was rid of foul little people like you Rawlston and tonight I might be just the man to do the world a favour!"

He lifted the revolver and pointed it straight at Rawlston's face, from which the blood instantly drained, blind terror sobering him in a second as he found himself looking down the barrel of the gun. He half screamed, turned and fled from the cottage, staggering down the path. The Major went after him, consumed with rage at this invasion of his home and the insults hurled at him by the man he so detested.

"And don't come back! Do you hear me? Don't you ever come back you disgusting little man!" he shouted as he raised the revolver and fired a shot into the air, speeding the terrified Rawlston on his way.

The booming crash from the gun jarred the Major back to reality. He looked at the revolver and lowered it, the stunned realisation of what he was holding and what he was doing suddenly registering and he was shocked that he would ever have gone so far with either Rawlston or indeed himself. He went back inside and locked the door. He looked again at the revolver and, with the importance of his original deadly intention fading, swiftly placed it back in the chest and locked it. He was seething with anger as he paced up and down. He had another drink of whisky and then sat at his desk. With shaking hands he tried to tie a salmon fly. Ten minutes later he tried tying another one. Having tied eight unacceptable efforts he found he was still fuming about Rawlston and decided the best thing he could do to calm himself would be to take his big, double handed salmon fly rod down to the Railway Pool and attempt to work off some steam and so, by 3.30a.m., that is precisely where he was.

It is extremely difficult to cast a salmon fly in the Railway Pool and, although the Major had it down to a fine art, it was going to be even more so in the dark. The railway embankment rose straight up from the river bank making any back cast difficult. To get any distance the Major had to lift his back cast high into the air and at an angle almost parallel to the river, so as not to catch the embankment, and then, squaring his shoulders to the river, pull the line that was out behind him down and around as he pushed the rod forward. With a release at precisely the right moment he could shoot the fly line out over the pool to land his fly within a few yards of the opposite bank. George Roberts was truly the master of the art of fly fishing the Railway Pool.

With anger burning deep within him he unhooked his favourite salmon fly from the long rod and began pulling the line that he was going to cast from the big brass reel. In the pitch black darkness he started flicking the fly line out and then pulled the rod upright to begin casting. Punching the line out across to the middle of the pool he kept pulling more line from the reel. He vented his anger by putting all the effort that he could into his casts, so much so that they became far from perfect, the fly whistling close past his ear on several occasions. Then, due to his misguided and extreme efforts, the fly caught hold of the embankment behind him. He was now so worked up and frustrated that, quite out of character, he completely lost his temper and went storming up the embankment in the darkness, feeling along the line to the fly, unhooked it and angrily reeled in the line that was lying like spaghetti all across the river bank.

Shaking with rage and exertion he began again. Further and further out he launched the fly and with each cast he put more and more effort into it. Sweat poured from him and his breath came shorter. Countless times the big rod powered back and forth as he pushed and pulled at it. As each thought of Rawlston came into his mind another powerful cast hissed out across the river. He was not attempting to catch anything, not fishing at all, just physically venting and assuaging his anger....and then it happened.

Enveloped in his wrath the Major had not felt the trembling vibrations, the approaching goods train being the furthest thing from his mind. Bursting from the tunnel the mechanical monster roared down the track behind him just as the Major, now almost out of strength, went into his back cast.....and the fly hooked itself to the train.

The weight that suddenly came onto the rod from this unexpected direction just about pulled him off his feet. Under violent pressure the big brass reel screamed a raucous song of complaint as it spewed the line out. The Major's eyes bulged and veins stood out on his face as he hung grimly onto to the rod and staggered backwards. The reel revolved faster and faster, enormous friction heating it to such a degree that it suddenly seized up and jammed. As the line was about to break the fly decided to detach itself from the train and the fly line came shooting forwards to fall in heaps around him at the edge of the water. He gasped, struggling for breath as both his mind and his body gave up and he collapsed backwards onto the bank, his head thumping down on the hard ground and there he unconsciously lay like a bundle of rags, whilst the train disappeared into the distance.

As he lay there, oblivious to the world around him, out in the pool the mighty salmon was dying. The poacher's deadly net had indeed done its work having closed its gills for those few moments too long. It had been drifting slowly downstream, barely able to fight against the current. But now its strong tail swept back and forth as it entered its death throes and the huge fish launched itself from the middle of the river in one final, powerful run, at the end of which it rammed itself into the river bank at the unconscious Major's feet, stone dead.

George Roberts lay there for hours, slipping in and out of consciousness.

The river lapped lazily at the bank as it eddied its way past him, the embankment behind and the trees opposite shielding him from the breeze. Not a soul stirred, the water flowing past being the only movement. At first light the clouds dispersed and all around him came to life. Rabbits began to move on the embankment, a duck and her brood swam past in echelon waiting for flies to hatch, a mink, dark and darting, hunted along the other bank and a small run of salmon head and tailed their way upstream.

As the Major lay motionless at the edge of the river, surrounded by nature, the sun came up and warmed him.

It was nine o'clock before he was found.

"Major! Come on, Major! Just breathe easy now. You're coming round."

The sun was so bright! A dog collar? A vicar? He lay there letting the increasing consciousness slowly clear his vision.

"Vicar? Is that really you vicar?"

"Yes it is Major. How are you feeling?"

"Not so good, old boy, not so good. Where am I?"

"You're at the Railway Pool and you've taken a nasty knock. I think you should just lie still."

There was blood at the back of George Roberts' head.

"But what happened, vicar? What am I doing here?"

"Now don't you worry Major, you'll remember in a while I'm sure. But for now you're going to have to lie still while I go and get some help. I don't want you to move, you may have concussion, so do you promise to lie there while I fetch someone?"

"I can hardly move anyway, old boy. But what on earth's going on? Why can't I remember?"

"There now Major, I'll be back with some help just as quickly as I can. You take it easy and whatever you do please don't move."

With that the vicar once again looked down at the Major lying there on the riverbank dressed in his military uniform with the enormous salmon lying at his feet. He shook his head in disbelief at the sight and then made off as fast as he could back to the village, where thankfully he ran straight into Sergeant Hughes. Word soon spread from those who overheard the vicar telling the Sergeant what had happened and within minutes people were rushing along the riverbank to help the Major. The policeman gently cushioned his head while they awaited the doctor and looked in amazement at the huge salmon. Soon a couple of dozen people were standing around the Major as the doctor tended to him. There had been gasps at the state he was in and more at the size of the fish. Although puzzled as to why he should be in uniform they agreed that the Major must have had an almighty battle, probably slipping at the last moment of his fight with the great fish and so getting himself into this predicament. Only the Major, they concurred, would have been able to land such a mighty salmon. They reeled in the line and carried his rod, the Major and the great fish back to his cottage where the doctor gave him some medication and put him to bed with strict instructions that he was not to stir.

Mrs.Ferzakerley, a local spinster, said she would stay to keep an eye on him, so everyone knew that he was in good hands. She bade the doctor goodbye, went upstairs and checked the Major who was now asleep and then looked around the cottage. She was horrified to see the state it was in with dirty dishes piled in the kitchen, dirty carpets, grubby curtains and thick dust lying everywhere. She set off home without delay and came back fifteen minutes later in her work clothes, laden with cleaning equipment. Rolling up her sleeves she took a deep breath and set about spring-cleaning the entire place.

Bert Hughes had taken charge of the salmon and, together with the large crowd that had gathered, proceeded in an orderly manner towards the village butcher's shop. The butcher, yet another taken aback by the size of the fish, prepared his scale for the weighing and with witnesses a many the great salmon was lifted onto it. As the weight was called out it brought exclamations of surprise.

"Well done the Major!" cried someone and the rest took up the shout. Sergeant Hughes arranged with the butcher that the salmon should be frozen until the Major was well enough to decide what to do with it and the crowd slowly dispersed, many in the direction of the Flying Start to spread the good news and drink to the Major's swift recovery.

The following day Rawlston, who was now suffering from a stinking cold as well as the remnants of his hangover, picked up his copy of the county newspaper and the headline that glared out at him completely and utterly ruined his day.

RIVER RECORD SHATTERED!
Major wins battle to land record 44lb. salmon!

The Response

The Arab

El Ahram Desert – 1135 hrs.

"See him! Look! Do you see him, my son?"

"Where Papa?"

"There, above the rise, turning to the right!"

"Which way is right Papa?"

"Allah is the way that is right," interjected a deeper voice.

"Please! Do not confuse the child! You see this way is to the right and this way is to the left."

"Where is he now Papa?"

"Ah! There he is, over there!" said the Sheikh, kneeling in the sand to let his son look along his arm and pointing finger. In the distance, out over the shimmering desert sands, a speck wheeled and turned.

"I see him Papa! I see him!"

The Sheikh turned to the Religious One.

"You see! My son! He can see! He can see!"

"Of course he can see, my Lord, we both know that Allah in his wisdom has given him two eyes. But can he see Allah?"

"Allah! Why must you always be talking of Allah? He will see Allah soon enough."

"And when will that be, O Great One?"

"When? Why...when Allah wishes to be seen, of course!"

"Of course, my Lord."

"He is coming Papa."

"Why must you always be talking to him of Allah? The child is but seven years old."

"Because it is never too early to learn the ways of Allah, my Lord."

"I know, you are right, but I ask you Religious One, is this the time? Is this the place?"

"Papa, he is coming!" cried the boy, tugging at his father's robes.

"Perhaps not, my Lord, but I shall never cease trying to teach your son the wisdom of Allah at every opportunity."

"Very well. I know you mean to do right. It is just that out here in the desert..."

"Papa!"

With the boy's excited cry the falcon arrived, speeding over them and arching into a tight turn. The Sheikh held out his arm and the sleek, powerful bird of prey flew straight to him and alighted.

"You see how free he is, my boy?" he asked his son as he hooded the bird.

"Out here it is his world, a world where he has the freedom of the skies, where he is the master, completely free to fly wherever he chooses. Ah, yes, it is such a wonderful thing, freedom."

"Papa?"

"Yes, my son."

"If he is free why do you put the hood on him?"

"So he will not fl... so the sun does not bother his eyes, that is why my son."

A vehicle that had been approaching the group of tents ground to a halt and a guttural voice called out. The Sheikh exchanged words with someone for a minute or two and then looked down at his son.

"Would you like to go to England, my boy?"

"What is England, Papa?"

"It is a country where they have a lot of green grass and it rains."

"I have seen grass, Papa."

"Not this much, nor this much rain, my son."

"Do we have to go, Papa?"

"I think we should. They have beautiful horses there you know and they are a different type to ours."

"OK Papa! We go to England to see the horses!"

The Sheikh flashed a winner's smile at the Religious One who, after a moment of reflection, wisely nodded his approval. They walked back to the tents, entering the largest one where the lunchtime feast was laid out. The Sheikh made sure that his son's meal was to his liking and then helped himself to the lamb, tearing pieces of it with his hands. Upon this signal the whole entourage began to talk and eat, knowing that the Sheikh was happy to be out in the desert with his son and his falcons.

"But, Papa."

"Yes, my son?"

The noise in the tent lowered as the child spoke.

"Papa, how can the sun bother the bird's eyes when he flies in the sun all the time?"

Everyone looked to the Sheikh, awaiting his wisdom, and this time he would indeed have to prove wise in his answer. However seizing upon inspiration he abandoned the idea of even trying to find one.

Instead he looked at the Religious One.

"You see how Allah works? My son takes after me. He is going to be extremely clever, you mark my words!"

"Allah be praised, my Lord," sighed the Religious One.

The Sheikh looked at the Religious One, smiled at his son, looked at the Religious One again and began to laugh, triggering laughter from everyone in the tent. Then he mischievously stopped laughing and everyone stopped in deference. He looked at his son, beaming at the child he loved, looked at the Religious One again and, with his dark eyes still twinkling with mischief, burst into laughter again and they all laughed with him.

The Aussie

Somewhere in the Australian Outback – Midday.

"Strewth! She's a hot one!"
Bill Boyd sat down at the bar and Mytle poured him a cold one.
"Hundred and ten today Billy Boy!"
"Think I might get drunk then."
"Need an excuse?"
"Nah, not really, just getting bored Myrtle."
He replaced the pint glass on the bar, empty. He had only picked it up seconds before. She began to refill it, knowing that only after the third would he begin to drink at a pace a human being could keep up with. She put the full glass on the bar and watched Bill pick it up and the beer flow down his throat. She was sure he swallowed, but it was hard to tell. She took the empty glass from him again and refilled it; he emptied it just as quick and gave out a long, astonishingly loud belch.
"If you didn't drink it so bleedin' fast you wouldn't have to be so disgusting."
"And if I drank it slow I wouldn't be able to belch like a star turn, now would I?"
They both laughed as others began entering the bar.
"Hey Bill, did you see this article about some gigantic auction they're holding over in England?"
"England?" echoed three or four voices.
"Well I know it's the other side of the world, but it must be real important to write about it over here, just have a look at this."
He handed over the paper and Bill began to read.
"Well blow me!"
"Not while there's a dog in the street!" said Myrtle and everyone fell about.
"Nah, listen to this: 'This important auction includes over one thousand lots of antiques, one hundred lots of farm implements, livestock including sheep, pigs and cattle, vintage cars, silverware, fine china, oil paintings and watercolours. More than 2500 lots in all. Full catalogue supplied on request.' Strewth, I could do with buying some of those farm implements and importing them and maybe some of the livestock too."
"You wouldn't be trying to kid us this doesn't have anything to do with your missus' love of antiques or your being hooked on vintage cars, would you?"
"Well I wouldn't deny it, Myrtle, but you must admit this does look interesting."
"Didn't it say that late entries would be accepted right up to sale time Bill? You could take your family heirloom over. It'd probably fetch a fortune over there, mate."
"You know, you might be right, it probably would."
"You're not seriously considering going to England just for an auction are you Bill?" asked Myrtle.

"Oh, I dunno, the missus has always wanted to go to England. Maybe we could sell the heirloom, buy some farm equipment and some antiques, ship everything back here and make ourselves some money."

Myrtle was aghast.

"Bill, you of all people don't need to make any money, remember?"

"Oh, yeah Myrtle, but that's really the missus's money. I mean I'd just like to make a little for myself."

"Make a little for yourself?" asked Myrtle, raising her eyebrows in disbelief at what she was hearing.

"Yeah, so what?"

Everyone in the bar was now staring at him.

"What the hell are you lot looking at?" he shouted at them disdainfully.

"It must be the heat!" yelled someone.

"I think we all need another bloody drink!" yelled someone else

As the days passed and the demand for catalogues became a flood the secretary had wanted to know how many Charles was having printed and had nearly fainted when he confessed to having ordered a thousand. One thousand? They had probably never ordered that amount in a whole year. She had become so upset and insistent they should tell Mr.Shipley that Charles had little option but to take her into his confidence. He had ended his talk with the somewhat flustered woman by saying,

"Look, you might as well know that I'm going to leave my job at the end of this auction, before Shipley can sack me. It's up to you what you want to do, but you're not responsible for anything that's going on, I am and the last thing I want to happen is for you to get into any trouble."

She was certainly seeing the young man in a different light now.

"But how many people are you reckoning on coming?"

"I really have no idea. You said you had almost two hundred enquiries last week."

"Yes, but it's nearly five hundred now."

The Yank

Reno, Nevada – 0542hrs.

The ground squirrel stood erect, eyeing the landscape.

Something was wrong out there, but it just couldn't figure out what it was. The crosshairs on the telescopic sight moved slowly up to its chest and stopped, the finger squeezed and the ground exploded about a foot to the right of the startled rodent, which vanished as swiftly as the loud 'crack' had come from the .22 rifle. Another one appeared further out, scurrying then stopping and this time the crosshairs moved slowly up its body to its head. Again a bullet hit the ground some twelve inches to the animal's right. The vehicle started up and began to crawl along the track. Twice more it stopped and each time a bullet hit the ground next to yet another surprised ground squirrel. Finally the vehicle came to the end of the track and turned onto the tarmac road.

It was 0630 when General Chuck Verbeer sat down to his breakfast of orange juice, ham & eggs, hash browns, bacon, sausage, tomato, wheat toast and black coffee. His wife, Hetty Joy, fussed in the kitchen knowing full well that the General, which was what she liked to call him even though he was retired, needed to have some peace early in the morning to enjoy his breakfast and read the paper.

Chuck Verbeer was the quintessential all-American general, a big powerful man with a granite face capable of looks that could strike fear into any soldier or that could just as easily break into a warm, morale boosting smile. On this particular morning he enjoyed his breakfast as usual and with his cup of black coffee moved to a comfortable seat in the window to continue reading the paper. In the distance the Truckee river tracked its course through the countryside, a formation of Canadian geese scarred the sky and, across the land of Washoe County that stretched away from the house, ground squirrels lived in peace, until the following morning.

The General frowned and re-read the advertisement, his frown deepening as he got up from the chair.

"Hetty Joy."

His wife instantly knew from the tone of his voice that something was going to happen. She appeared from the kitchen wiping her hands on her apron and looked at his giant outline framed in the window.

"Hetty Joy, honey, we might be going to England."

That was all he said and all he needed to say. His wife withdrew back into the kitchen. She knew that when he said they 'might' be going it was pretty definite they would be going and that he was warning her they could take off at any time. He hadn't even needed to tell her their destination. It wouldn't matter whether it was the North Pole or the Sahara Desert, wherever it was Hetty Joy would have it covered. So many forays to unknown destinations over the years had honed her insight into what to prepare for their needs. She enjoyed being the General's complete backup system and she never failed him.

"Hey Harry!" said her husband into the phone, "How you doing? Listen is that kid of yours free this morning? Something's come up. Oh good, tell him I'll make it worth his while, OK?"

He paced slowly up and down, thinking while he waited for young John to arrive. Even before they greeted each other some little time later John knew that the General would probably be wanting him to ferret out the kind of information he'd been supplying for a while now. His elder brother worked in the Reno Police Department and so, along with the contacts the General had given him, he had access to a bank of information from which he could find out just about anything. He listened as the General ran through the detail of what he wanted and promised to get it done as fast as possible.

Back outside he turned to ask a question.

"Shoot any ground squirrels this mornin', General?"

"Yep, seventeen."

John nodded in admiration and looked out across the land.

"And they're all still out there just a runnin' around?"

"They sure are, right as rain."

John shook his head.

"People wouldn't believe how you go out and do that General, you know, the way you deliberately miss them all the time."

"Well no one's asking them to believe it because you're not going to be telling anyone, now are you?"

His look said it all.

Young John laughed.

"You know your secret's safe with me, General."

"It'd better be, son," replied the General, smiling.

"It'd better be."

The Jap

Nagano Prefecture – 1500hrs.

Descending like a Zero attacking a convoy Hiroyuki Takada pointed them straight down the mountain. Hunched over the front of his skis he steeled himself into the long shus and descended at increasing speed, his legs taking the jarring bumps and jolts whenever the mountain fed them to him. He sped between two groups of those who had stopped on the run to rest, only allowing himself to wander from the straight line with two long, curving turns before ending up crouched in the glide position on the flat run in to the lodge where his friend was waiting.

After taking all the skiing paraphernalia from him in order as he first released his skis, took his goggles, ski hat and gloves off and then removed his ski boots to put on the winter shoes that were provided, his friend turned and they walked one behind the other to the parking lot, stopping next to the unusual sight of a Rolls Royce with a roof rack.

Takada got into the back seat whilst the skis were fitted onto the rack and the rest of the gear stowed in the boot, after which the other man, now wearing a chauffeur's peaked hat, got into the driver's seat.

"You're still a madman," he said, glancing in the mirror as he started the Rolls.

"Shh! Don't tell everybody," said Takada, smiling.

"Everybody already knows." said his 'chauffeur', "Why don't you act your age? Coming down the mountain like that, you'll kill yourself one day at that speed."

Takada picked up the paper to read as they made their way home.

A Bullet train passed them next to the highway, making their progress seem somewhat sedate.

"Another madman," said the chauffeur, "Why does everyone have to rush all the time in Japan?"

"I have news for you my friend," said Takada, looking up from the newspaper.

"Don't tell me you've finally arranged a date for me with that movie starlet."

"No, but you know I could if you wanted me to."

They looked at each other through the mirror, the chauffeur muttering that it wouldn't really be necessary.

"We are going to England my friend, that is the news."

"England? But we've only just come back from Europe! We could have thrown a stone at it out of the plane just three weeks ago."

"Well I feel like some Shakespeare," said Takada, ignoring the tirade.

"You look like Shakespeare and I am no longer your friend."

"Oh, not again," said the smiling Takada knowing full well their long association would assuredly survive and so, with his 'ex-friend' grumbling about the amount of work he would have to do handling the packing and travel arrangements and why they couldn't have gone to England when they had been in Europe in the first place, they progressed homeward.

Charles had managed to finish the lotting up of the sale items for the printer to be able to produce the catalogue in good time. In the massive amount of worldwide advertising there was going to be for the auction he and Nancy had put the supposed number of lots at a ridiculous two thousand five hundred with the intent of arousing the greatest possible interest. But having now taken in a huge amount of items on top of Shipley's original five hundred, along with those from the farm in the next valley, Charles had surprised himself by reaching the dizzying figure of two thousand eight hundred and forty six lots not including items that were yet to be entered by people at the last minute.

Even the fastest auctioneer, selling at a rate of 150 lots per hour and enduring a long eight hour day, would take more than two days to sell everything. But Shipley normally sold at only around 90 lots per hour and sometimes less than that. To make matters worse Charles had thrown some spokes into Shipley's wheel by deliberately cataloguing many items in a somewhat inept and inaccurate way. He had also altered some of Shipley's own descriptions by either making deliberate mistakes in them or by placing the wrong descriptions against the wrong lot numbers.

Early on in the process he had taken a vase from its box and had been struck by the feeling there was something familiar about it. A little while later he had come across a watercolour painting that he was sure he had seen before. Finally there had been a china tea service in blue and gold. He recognised it immediately as he had taken it in himself about a year previously from an elderly lady and it had not done well for her, making barely thirty pounds. Yet now Shipley had an estimated price against it of nearly six times that figure. Being curious, Charles searched back through the catalogues of the previous two years and traced over seventy items that had passed through their hands once before and were to be sold again in this auction.

This was not so unusual as buyers sometimes did a bit of dealing, placing items they had previously purchased back into auction to try and make themselves a profit and this was perfectly legal, but with these items there was one substantial difference.

They were all under the name 'Rubicon'.

He pondered this mystery for a while, kept checking the old sales records and found that all the items had been sold for extremely low prices against their original estimates in the paperwork. How could Shipley sell an item once and then still have it for sale? Money had been paid out to each vendor, so they had definitely been sold and yet here they were again, lots of them. He looked up the description of the old lady's tea service. It simply read: 'A tea service'.

Now that was odd. If Shipley had wanted to get the best price for it the description should have read something like: 'A superb Paragon transferware forty piece tea service in Royal Blue and Gold comprising...." Just cataloguing it as 'a tea service' almost guaranteed it wouldn't make any money.

The penny finally dropped when he checked one of the oil paintings. He located the original sale it had purportedly been sold in some eighteen months previously and found that the catalogue description simply read: 'An oil painting.'

This did the painting no justice at all as it depicted a beautiful country scene with horses ploughing beside a small stream and a thatched cottage with smoke rising from the chimney. It was signed and in an impressive gilt frame, but had previously sold for only two hundred pounds. Now it was up for sale with the full description it warranted, at an estimated value of two thousand pounds.

"It's illegal Nancy." Charles informed her on the phone.

"What must have been going on is that Shipley has been substituting much poorer quality things for those he was originally supposed to be selling, stealing the original item and reselling it later for a huge profit. No wonder I used to hear such rows with angry vendors when I first started with the firm."

"What should we do about it?"

"I don't know, I suppose I should go to the police, but they might come straight in and stop the auction before it even starts."

"Can't you go to them with it as a hypothetical situation and see what they advise?"

"I suppose I could, but I'm sure there are a lot more things than I've found so far that Shipley has entered, so maybe the police would want to wait until we've researched exactly how many of these items there are."

"Maybe they'll want to catch him in the act as well. I think you should go and see them just before the auction, that way you can keep your job for these last few weeks."

"Alright, I will, but I'll have to do this hypothetical thing until they agree to let the auction go ahead."

The Cornishman

Julius Polperro read the advertisement again.

Perhaps it was the buccaneering, piratical side of his lineage that sparked his interest in the thought of unknown treasure, but it clearly stated in the advertisement that there were 'Assorted lots comprising silverware and locked boxes possibly containing jewellery and precious metal'.

Not really the regular kind of thing that he was used to finding at auctions where normally he spent his time buying odd assortments of antiques and bric-a-brac and selling them to market traders and antique shops. It kept him solvent and he enjoyed travelling around the country buying and selling.

'China, pottery, paintings, artefacts.'

Artefacts?

He was definitely not going to miss this one.

The Lancashire Lads

The Grubb brothers lived in a sprawling farmhouse in the Pennines where they farmed 300 acres of mixed dairy.

Horace and Maurice Grubb inherited the farm they had lived in all their lives from their parents and had done well over the years from their astute management of it. For them money was not one of life's problems and so with it they collected just about everything. The rambling farm buildings were full of all sorts of things from pure junk to old cars, a fire engine, antiques of all descriptions, garden statues, lathes, pieces of furniture, a trap for a pony and spare parts for probably anything mechanical that had ever been invented.

They were strange, round, jovial men who wore flat caps and spectacles, the lenses of Maurice's being particularly thick due to his short sightedness. Both were bachelors and seemed quite content to stay that way. Their manner was bumbling and kindly and they worked as a team as they went around the country in their spare time buying odd things at house sales and country auctions. One of them would spot something and they would consult. Whether they knew what the item actually was or even its value was not important. What was important was whether they both liked it and, if they did, they would have a go at buying it and they both very much liked the sound of the advertisement that Maurice was reading out.

The Scotsman

The Laird of the Highlands sipped his tea as he read the newspaper, now this really was an interesting piece.

Willie Laird, known to all as 'the Laird of the Highlands', was the owner of two small supermarkets in Invernesshire and was the kind of man who might be interested in buying some livestock and maybe some antiques if he thought he could make a pound or two out of them. He became quite excited at the thought of going south wearing the kilt and playing the pipes to announce to the Sassenachs that he was coming and then giving them a good thrashing in the sale room so he could bring some of the better things back to Scotland.

He decided there and then that he would go to England and attend the auction and that he would take his two sons Hamish and Rory with him and that the three of them would take the train.

The Flying Scotsman.

Mickey picked up the phone.

He listened to the voice on the other end.

"No, we're just a pub, we don't have any accommodation I'm afraid."

He listened again.

"No, we don't do bed and breakfast either, the only accommodation here is occupied by me and the family, I'm sorry."

He listened again.

"No we certainly will not!"

He put the phone down hard.

"Some idiot wants us to move out so he can stay here luv, what do you think of that?"

"Cheek of some people, anyway why on earth would they call us and not one of the hotels down the valley?"

"I dunno, very strange, bloke was some kind of foreigner so maybe that was it."

But other people's phones had been ringing all over the village for some days and the enquiries were always the same, people were looking for accommodation.

Mrs.Ferzakerley had agreed to take two people in on condition they paid her cash and rooms had also been rented from the butcher, the postman, the owner of the general store, the plumber, the roofer, the electrician, the roadman and a number of others. As the village became saturated the enquiries had spread further afield. Down the valley the Tudor Arms and the Somerville Hotel had rapidly filled with bookings. The demand for accommodation was accelerating, spreading in an ever widening circle with the village at its centre.

Dirk and Terry entered the pub for their lunchtime drink.

"How do, Mickey, the usual please."

As Mickey pulled their pints the conversation turned to the goings on.

"What do you reckon to all the people wanting to come here Mickey?"

"All what people?"

"All them what's making bookings and arranging to stay in Little Saddlington at the end of the month."

"Strange you should say that, I had a bloke on the blower this morning trying to rent rooms off me. Asked if me and the wife would move out so he could move in. I ask you."

"Well seemingly people are paying good rates if they can get a room. Might be worth you thinking about."

"Nah, I mean who would ever pay enough to get us to move out? It's silly. Anyway, why does everyone suddenly want to come here of all places?"

"For the auction mate, they say it's going to be a real big 'un."

"Yeah, we hear they're even going to put a marquee up on the village green for it. People comin' from all over they reckon, going to be quite a busy old time."

"Oh?" said Mickey, thinking to himself 'who would be supplying the drink for all these people? Who would be catering at this marquee? Maybe he should go and see Eric Shipley?'

The phone rang.

"Hello, the Flying Start. Oh, it's you again, look I already told you we weren't prepared to move out. Yes, but you must be able to find somewhere, surely? Have you tried the Tudor Arms and the Somerville? They're both full? Well I never, look I'd like to help you but it really is quite out of the question and I'm very sorry..."

The voice on the phone interrupted and went on for some time.

"Alright, but who would help us run the pub while we're living out? What do you mean 'you will'?"

The voice carried on with Mickey interjecting occasionally.

"Well OK then, let's say we did move out and you did take over our accommodation. You'd have to pay us enough to convince us to go you know, so what almighty sum would you be offering then?"

The two poachers were nodding at him as vigorously as Mrs.Mickey was shaking her head in annoyance. The voice continued and Mickey's jaw dropped open.

"Blimey!"

The voice continued.

"Blimey!" he said again.

"Look are you sure? It seems an awful lot. Well, alright, if you say so, and it's cash is it? We don't really have an option then do we? When will you arrive? And your name? And can I have a phone number to get hold of you on?"

He waited as the voice continued.

"Blimey!" he said as he slowly replaced the phone. There was absolute silence. Everyone in the pub was looking at him, including Mrs.Mickey.

"Mickey, please tell me you haven't! Don't tell me we've got to move out, please!"

"Listen luv, the man's coming and he's going to pay us so much I simply couldn't turn him down. We've got to accept his offer."

"No, we don't! We don't have to accept anything at all and you know it!"

"But think of the money, luv, It's on top of our normal earnings here. We've got to go. We can't afford to turn him down and anyway I've told him I accepted."

"Mickey, you really are the limit! I've got to move out of my own house and give it to some stranger? It's not on! Have you taken leave of your senses?"

"Luv it's a real lot of money, honest."

"Well how much is a 'real lot of money' you idiot!"

"He's going to pay us…"

Mickey stopped as he realised the entire pub was leaning towards him to hear the amount, so instead he whispered it into his wife's ear.

"Blimey!" said Mrs.Mickey, "Was he serious?"

"He said the money would be here before he would and he'd like everything ready just to walk into."

"Well then," she sighed resignedly, "I guess I better start packing. How many of them will there be?"

"Just the two of them the feller said."

"Where's he comin' from then, Mickey?" asked Terry.

"You're not going to believe this," said Mickey looking around the bar.

"But he said he's coming from Australia."

"Blimey!" they all exclaimed.

Somebody dropped a glass.

At Rubicon & Shipley the phone was now going non-stop.

Each time the secretary put it down it rang again and every call was an enquiry about the auction and every caller wanted a catalogue. She took their names, addresses and phone numbers and kept a check on the number of enquiries she had received.

"Mr.Montgomery I've had twenty seven requests for catalogues already today and it's only two o'clock. Look at the amount of postal enquiries that have come in this morning and the phone just never stops. I'm getting really worried."

"Worried, why?"

"We're past a thousand enquiries and there's still almost three weeks to go to the auction and we won't have room for all these people in the hall. I'm sure Mr.Shipley's going to find out. I'm so worried Mr.Montgomery. What are we going to do?"

"A thousand? But I've only ordered a thousand catalogues in total."

"I know and already we've run out of them before they've arrived. You better do something. And how are we going to hide all this from Mr.Shipley? Oh, I just know we're going to get into terrible trouble!"

"Well, we'll just have to work out of my place at night and keep all of these enquiries out of Shipley's sight. I better call the printer and get the order increased. What do you reckon will be the final number of catalogues we'll need? Two thousand?"

The secretary began to cry.

Converging

Chuck Verbeer was not a happy General.

Initially pleased to find that his journey had ended in such a charming English village he'd then had great trouble finding somewhere for himself and Hetty Joy to stay. Having also carefully examined the auction catalogue on their long flight across 'The Pond' he had realised there was something wrong with such a huge auction being held in such a tiny village.

As a first priority he had located Charles whom he had inveigled with some difficulty into a game of golf on the village's tiny nine hole course, ignoring all protests about his not having enough time to play due to the impending auction. They had completed three holes, having levelled each one, and were out of sight of the clubhouse when Charles was about to play his second shot into the fourth green. As he took his practice swing however the General stooped and picked up his ball.

Charles was puzzled, little did he realise that a great moment of truth had arrived.

"Er, General, that's my ball."

"Yes, son, yes it is."

"Is there some kind of problem?"

"Problem? Well, let me tell you. Yes, there certainly is a problem. You see there's this little hick town, that's a problem. Then there's this dumb auction, that's another problem and right now there's this game of golf. They are all one great big problem to me."

"Whatever do you mean, General?"

In one swift, powerful movement the General's number four iron moved from the vertical to the horizontal position forced up between Charles' legs, blade uppermost. Chuck Verbeer's powerful forearms exerted such an upward pressure on the shaft that Charles squealed as he found the golf club had him firmly pinioned by the crotch, front and back.

"Problems, son! Problems! That's what I mean! I've got a load of them and now so have you!"

Charles attempted to wriggle off the club, but the General held firm.

"You got me to come halfway around the world on false pretences! A misrepresentation you could call it! So do tell me how come such a huge auction is taking place way out here in the boondocks and why I should be reading about this con of an auction of yours in a newspaper in Reno!"

He looked down and then back up at Charles' straining face.

"Open my eyes, son, open them do or this could be the end of life as you know it!"

"But it's a great auction, General! Why there are all kinds of valu...Aaagh!"

"I have patience, son, but none for you right now!" said Chuck Verbeer as he lifted Charles up onto his tiptoes.

"Now is the time for honesty, son, believe me!"

"Aaagh! Alright! You win General! Please stop!"

"You give me one wrong steer you young pipsqueak and I'll start again," said the General, releasing him from the club.

Charles moved gingerly around, rubbing his crotch, and began to tell his story. Faster and faster it came out and the more he spoke the more the General's face began to change. The granite began to slowly soften as his level of understanding of the situation increased by leaps and bounds. For some ten minutes Charles babbled on as they stood there facing each other. The tension was evaporating fast and Charles found himself talking as if pouring his heart out to some lifelong confidante. The more the General said 'I see' in such an agreeable way the easier Charles found it to tell him the whole sorry tale.

Whilst he was in full flow however the General suddenly interrupted.

"Quiet! Look!"

He was pointing over Charles' shoulder, his gaze fixed somewhere in the distance. Charles turned to see what he was looking at.

They were coming out of the East.

Eight men encased in metal travelling at 450 knots, exhaust plumes tracking down from the clouds behind them. In close formation they came arrowing along the valley, hanging in the sky for a few seconds as if poised to attack and then, as the noise from their engines increased to a deafening roar, they suddenly closed the distance and bore down upon the two specks standing out on the fairway. Charles instinctively ducked and pressed his hands to his ears as the fighters came blasting overhead.

The General stood his ground, unflinching, immovable, his eyes covering every possible detail in the seconds the planes were above them. As he caught a glimpse of one of the pilots he yelled out something that could have been some ancient battle cry, but it was drowned out by the shattering crescendo from the thundering jet engines. And then, as suddenly as they had come, they were gone, exhaust plumes tell-taling the path of their exit back up into the heavens, leaving only rumbling reverberations echoing around the valley to attest to their passing.

Charles removed his hands from his ears and looked at the General's now radiant, beaming expression. It was the look of a person who had completely assumed a mantle of warm, fatherly ambience.

Friendliness was all pervading.

"Well, well, well," chuckled the General, "Her Majesty's Royal Air Force. Hah! Those goddamn Fly Boys!"

He slapped Charles on the back, knocking most of the wind out of him.

"It's going to be alright, son, everything's going to be just fine, don't you worry. You see, God is in his heaven and the enemy, the aggressor, shall not win. The only problem I sometimes have these days is identifying just who exactly the enemy really is."

He looked at Charles who was coughing and spluttering as he tried to suck air back into his lungs whilst shaking his head to get rid of the ringing in his ears.

"But it certainly isn't you, is it? Whatever in the wide, wide world of sports is the matter with you now? I think we've had enough golf for today, Mr.Montgomery, what you and I need are a couple of good stiff drinks. Big one's! That'll set us up. So let's make on back to the clubhouse and see what they've got in the bar. What d'you say?"

"But General, I don't...I mean..."

"Now then, son, I told you not to worry."

And so with Charles trying desperately to explain that he didn't really drink, the newly benevolent, but equally determined Chuck Verbeer picked up both golf bags in one hand, locked the hapless Charles under his other arm and strode briskly off towards the clubhouse, glancing back just once to look again at the point of departure of the Royal Air Force. Chuckling to himself he shook his head as he marched along, not impeded in the slightest by either Charles or the golf bags as, armed with the information Charles had given him, he was in a much happier frame of mind.

General Chuck Verbeer was now a man on a mission.

The Flying Start had never done business like it.

Mickey had to get onto the brewery and order kegs of beer and, seizing the opportunity, he was now doing bar food all day long, which was going down a treat. He also had an idea that he ought to be selling sandwiches, cold sausages and soft drinks out on the village green for the auction's viewing days. Luckily he and Mrs.Mickey had been able to move in with some friends up the street. It was a bit crowded, but it was only going to be for a week or so. He was still able to run everything in the pub without much problem and had drafted in a couple of local ladies to help prepare the food. Every so often he and his wife would give each other a slightly amazed look as they watched their daily takings mounting, but it was hard work and their efforts deserved reward.

On this particular evening the pub was filled with more than the usual crowd. Stories about the auction and the people coming to it abounded and there was even a rumour that a couple of Japanese were staying at the Somerville. Folk with caravans and hordes of people with backpacks and tents were arriving daily, so many that the local Bobby was having great difficulty working out where he was going to allow everyone to stop.

"Where's your geezer then Mickey?" asked Dirk.

Mickey took the money for some drinks and opened the till.

"I haven't heard a word from him since that phone call."

"Well, when did he say he'd be here?"

"He didn't. Just said the money would be here before he would. I hope he turns up otherwise my life will be hell."

He glanced at Mrs.Mickey and was met with a severe look.

"Are you sure he was coming from Australia?"

"Yeah, but I must say now that time's wearing on," he looked at his wife again, "maybe it was Austria he said!"

A dishcloth hit him in the side of the head.

"'Ere, if he doesn't turn up can me and the 'Erp move in for the week?" asked Bob looking expectantly at Mrs.Mickey.

"No, you most certainly cannot!" she exclaimed in alarm and disappeared into the back as the laughter escalated.

"You did get his name, didn't you Mick?"

"Yeah I've got it on a note here somewhere. Here it is, he's a Mr.Boyd, a Mr.Bill Boyd."

"That must be me!"

The noise in the pub died as everyone strained to see the voice's owner and, like the waters of the Red Sea before Moses and the Children of Israel, the crowd parted from the bar to the doorway and there, large as life, stood Bill Boyd.

"Billy Boyd's my name everyone and I'm pleased to meet you all. Sorry if I'm a bit late, but it's a bloody long way to come from Australia. I'd just like to say that we're not going to be the slightest trouble to any of you while we're here and that we'd like to count all of you as our friends. Oh, and this is my missus."

He turned and through the open doorway stepped Bill Boyd's wife into the vacuum created by a united intake of pub breath. She was absolutely stunning. An elegant and beautiful blonde with blue eyes and the most unbelievable figure, the main feature of which was a pair of 38's encased in a flimsy, open topped cotton dress.

Nobody moved, nobody breathed, they froze with their eyes glued to the 38's.

You could have heard a pin drop.

Somebody dropped a glass.

"She's the ex-Miss Australia and in case any of you are in any doubt this little beauty belongs to me, so don't go getting any ideas! She is quite definitely Mrs.Bill Boyd, aren't you doll?"

She nodded.

Still no one breathed.

He looked around at all the stunned faces.

"Now then, which one of you is the guy I spoke to over the phone?"

"Er, that's me, I'm Mickey," said Mickey shaking himself out of the spell. Bill and his missus strode forward and crossed the parted Red Sea with their hands extended.

"Pleased to meet you, Mickey."

They shook hands across the bar.

"Have you got that stuff for Mickey, doll?"

His missus, all eyes still on her, dipped into her bag and produced a large brown envelope. Bill motioned for her to give it to Mickey.

"Sorry the money didn't arrive before us, well it nearly did, didn't it? It's all there Mickey and it's all in cash. Pounds Sterling. Is that alright?"

"Er, yeah, yeah that's fine Bill. Oh, this is my wife."

As they shook hands Bill was just beginning to feel a little uneasy at the continuing silence.

"Well our bags are outside so if…"

"I'll get them!" said Bob to the disbelief of the entire pub.

"OK mate, thank you. Now then Mickey as every person in this bar is now a friend of ours, me and my missus would like to buy every single one of them a drink!"

And that was it, they closed in on the Australian couple, introducing themselves, asking questions, getting as near to the 38's as they dared (well the men anyway) and Mickey and his staff started serving them.

"I drink beer myself," announced Bill.

Mickey gave him the first pint he pulled and Bill looked at it.

"Bit dark this beer of yours isn't it, Mick?"

"That's one of the best pints you can get around here Bill."

"What do you think doll?"

His missus looked at the pint and shrugged.

"I'll definitely give it a go shall I?"

She looked at him with one eyebrow raised and held three fingers up to Mickey.

"Yeah, she's right, I'm going to need three of these Mick, so set 'em up would you please?"

His missus' smile broadened as Bill put the pint glass to his mouth and began to drink. As the glass tilted up the noise in the pub began to die again. The beer disappeared and Bill reached for the second pint just as Mickey put it on the bar. The talking died completely as the second pint flowed out of sight and Bill got hold of the third and gave it the same treatment.

He replaced the glass on the bar, looked at his missus who looked back at him expectantly and then, to his missus' knowing nod of approval, he gave out the longest, loudest belch anyone in the pub had ever heard and everyone burst into laughter.

"Not bad, not bad at all, bit different this beer of yours Mick and it's a bit warm, can't you make it colder for me?"

"Well, I…"

"Never mind, just kidding, now then, come on everyone! Drink up!"

Bill's missus smiled. He was a hit just like he always was everywhere they went and just like he always had been with her. She knew he was in his element and that made her more than happy. Bill leaned across the bar to Mickey.

"You know I reckon if we put my missus to work behind your bar this place will be the busiest pub in England."

Mickey looked at the 38's and then at Bill's missus' face and was embarrassed to find her looking straight back at him, smiling proudly.

"Behind the bar?"

"Yeah, she's real good at pub work, Mick, after all that's where I found you, didn't I doll? She'll pull 'em in from miles around, mind you, you'll definitely have to get a bigger cash register mate!"

The large black limousine slid quietly up to the village green and came to a halt. The men putting up the marquee stopped work to look at it. The front doors opened and two men dressed just like Lawrence of Arabia got out of it. The rear door opened and out came a small boy followed by a much more imposing looking man, who was also dressed in fine white robes, but with gold around his head dress.

This was definitely an Arab.

They stared at him.

"Ah, what a beautiful place, such greenery, such trees, such nice people and so cool, even with the sun shining."

The Sheikh found this quaint English village to be most pleasing, if a little small.

"We still have nowhere to stay tonight my Lord."

"Ah, cannot Allah save us? Where shall we make our camp? Here in this great tent?" said the Sheikh as they walked towards it.

"It won't be up by tonight, mate, and anyway rules is no one's allowed to sleep in 'ere."

"Thank you my good man!" said the Sheikh turning to the Religious One.

"What did he say?"

"He said we cannot stay here, my Lord."

The Sheikh walked to the middle of the green smiling in acknowledgement to people as they moved back in awe of this strange looking man of the desert. As his son skipped about on the grass he looked around.

"Does not anyone know of a place where we can stay?"

They all shook their heads.

"Everywhere's full for miles around here."

The Sheikh had to come up with some kind of accommodation for them and quickly. He stroked his chin thoughtfully, looked around and out of the corner of his eye spied a building that might possibly suit without giving any indication that he had seen it and quickly looked at the ground as if suddenly wrapped in studious thought.

"Religious One you believe that Allah watches over us, do you not?"

"Indeed he does at all times, your Greatness."

"And that he will watch over us this night, despite the fact that we have not been able to find ourselves a place to stay?"

"Most assuredly, Highness."

"Well then in Allah we place our trust! We put our faith in him!"

The two men echoed him, crying together,

"In Allah we place our trust! We put our faith in him!"

The Sheikh placed his hand over his eyes and began to turn himself around. He turned twice one way, stopped and slowly turned almost three times back the other way. He stopped and, with his hand still covering his eyes, held his other arm out and pointed.

"This is the place where we shall stay this night!"

Together they looked to where he was pointing. There in the distance, away up on the gently sloping hill, was a large house.

"Please someone! Tell me what place this is that Allah has shown to us!"

"That's the manor house on Rawlston Manor Estate," said one of the people standing nearby.

"But you can't stay there, it's private."

"Privacy, my good man, is but a state of mind that can be made to vanish as quickly as water from our desert. Thank you indeed for your help good people and may Allah watch over you as he so truly watches over us!"

With that they walked back to the car, disappeared into it and drove off to the end of the village green. The limousine turned and as it came back the rear window had been wound down and the Sheikh was waving to everyone shouting,

"Allah be praised! May Allah watch over you!"

Some of those he passed actually found themselves waving back at his infectious enthusiasm.

"I've seen it all now," said one of the workmen, "This place has gone bloody mad. A-rabs, I ask you, bleedin' A-rabs! Whatever next?"

As the limousine arrived at the front entrance Geoffrey Rawlston was sitting in his study. Upon hearing the car he came out into the hall, opened the front door and jumped at the Arabian sight that confronted him on the doorstep.

"You are the owner?"

"Yes. Yes, I am."

"We wish to stay here for some time, please be so good as to name the price."

"What! No you bloody don't! This is my house and it's private! You're not staying here! Go on, push off! Who the bloody hell do you think you are?"

Rawlston made to push them back off the doorstep, in a flash curved daggers were brandished inches from his face by the two on either side of the one who had been speaking.

The Sheikh rolled his eyes to the heavens.

"I am Sheikh Ahmed Layel Hoochnaya bin-Charachd-Elfaharsi! The Voice of the Desert! Sacred Servant of Allah! Provider to his People! Teacher of his Wisdom and," he opened his eyes and glared at Rawlston, "Ruler of All he Surveys! Now what is the price to stay in this house for the duration of this, er..."

"Auction, your Grace."

"Yes, auction."

"Look, this is my home!"

The daggers came even closer.

"But you would be welcome in my home for no payment at all, as are all the peoples who wander upon the earth. What is the price?"

"I can't, I mean, really, you must understand..."

"Silence! We shall not wait longer for I can see that you are a difficult man. As you will not give us the price..." the Sheikh snapped his fingers and the one who was not the Religious One produced a flat bag from within his robes and handed it to him without moving his eyes from Rawlston or removing the dagger from his face.

The Sheikh produced a fistful of money from the bag.

"This is what we offer to stay in your house!"

Rawlston looked in amazement at the large wad of notes in the Sheikh's hand.

"Take it or we go!"

A shaken Geoffrey Rawlston took the money and the Arabs walked past him into the hallway and on into the lounge. He ran after them.

"But don't you want to count what you've just given me?"

The Sheikh made a dismissive gesture.

"We would like to eat now."

"Eat?"

"Yes, you do eat I suppose?"

Rawlston nodded dumbly.

"Well have you any lamb?"

"Lamb?"

"Yes, it is a small sheep."

"Oh, lamb! Yes, I'll get some lamb! You just hang on here and I'll organise some food!"

The Sheikh sighed.

Rawlston's brain had finally overcome the shock and shifted into gear as he realised how valuable these 'guests' of his might be considering the large amount of money they had just furnished him with.

"Good, we will look to establish ourselves in your house, find our places to sleep and await your call to dine."

"Dine? Yes, of course, I'll just be a little while your, er…"

He backed out of the room half bowing and left them to get his car and go shopping. After he had gone the Sheikh looked at those with him.

"A pathetic individual, he can be bought. He will be no trouble and Allah has provided us with a roof over our heads. Come! Let us investigate our new home!"

Despite the fact that it was midsummer the Sheikh felt cold in the house and his two men soon had a fire going in the lounge, fortunately in the fire place, which they would keep alight for the entire length of their stay. Then they climbed the stairs to choose their bedrooms. The Sheikh picked the best one and his men removed all Rawlston's clothes and possessions from it, taking them downstairs to a small room just off the kitchen. The two women in the kitchen, Rawlston's staff, were alarmed at first and then amused when they saw what the Arabs were doing. The two bodyguards brought a small bed into the Sheikh's room so the child could sleep in the same room as his father and then they took bedrooms for themselves, but outside the Sheikh's door they made a kind of sitting place on the floor of the landing with cushions and pillows. This would be occupied by one of them whenever the Sheikh slept and woebetide anyone trying to get past.

The Sheikh's young son looked out of the window of their new bedroom.

"Papa, why do they make those lines across the land?"

"Lines? Where my son? Oh those, they are walls and fences. That is how they keep their animals together by placing them in the spaces in between so they cannot get out."

"But we do not have lines Papa and our animals stay together."

"Yes, that is right, but here they do things differently to our way at home."

"Our animals are free Papa, their animals are not."

"I believe you are right in what you say my son."

The Sheikh put his arm around his boy as they stood looking out of the window.

"Their animals are not as free as ours. There is a lot of freedom in our desert, is there not?"

"Yes Papa, when will we see some horses?"

"Oh the horses, quite soon I hope, quite soon."

"I will look for them Papa."

The Sheikh went into the bathroom.

"I can see them Papa!"

"What can you see my child?"

"Horses running! They are running and running!"

The Sheikh came swiftly back out of the bathroom.

"Where are they my son?"

"There they are Papa! Out there!"

The Sheikh looked, but he could see no horses, the fields were empty apart from a few cows in one some distance away.

"Out there my son?"

"Yes Papa, the horses are there and they are running because they are free!"

"The horses are free? It is a game, yes?"

"No, Papa! It is not a game!"

The Sheikh was startled by this scolding and hugged his son to him as, with their faces pushed together against the window pane, he gazed out at the fields trying to understand.

"Then explain to your Papa what you mean, my boy, for I do not understand you."

"You must look and you will see the horses Papa."

"Ah, they are imaginary horses?"

"Papa!" said his son, chiding his father's lack of seriousness.

"Alright, alright, the horses are there, but I cannot see them so you must show them to me."

"Oh Papa, why can't you see them? The men come and they take away the lines and all the land becomes as one, just like our desert, and there are the horses, running and running because they are free! See them, the big grey, the black and the white one running free across the land!"

"Take away the lines? Running free?"

As the realisation of what his son was trying to explain dawned upon him the tranquil scene in front of the Sheikh began to transform dramatically. His eyes glazed over and he became almost bewitched as he looked out across the fields that stretched away into the distance. For a few magical moments he

41

dreamed with his son and together they could see a herd of wild horses galloping across the land led by a magnificent stallion, their hooves pounding the earth as it sped underneath them. There were no walls or fences to check them as on they came, so clear in every detail, their heads moving rhythmically, their hot breath streaming, their eyes staring, their flanks rippling, the dust rising behind them. A herd of noble horses thundering their way across the English landscape, the majestic power of them as consummate as it was mesmerising.

Snapping out of it the Sheikh kissed and hugged his son, stood up, put his head back and gave out a very great and long cry, shattering the quiet in the house. Within seconds his two men had burst into the room, daggers at the ready. The Sheikh collapsed to his knees, sobbing and pointing to his son. The two looked at the boy.

"But my Lord, the child is well! What has happened?"

The Sheikh nodded, still breathing in sobs.

"My Lord," the Religious One stooped beside him, greatly concerned.

"Are you dying?"

The Sheikh shook his head, gulped in some air and said,

"Allah is here! He is here in this very room! You must bless me Religious One and you must bless the boy! Immediately!"

"Yes, my Lord!"

The Religious One did as he was commanded and raised his voice in ancient Arabic prayer for the blessings of Allah as the Sheikh and his son knelt before him in Rawlston's bedroom.

Sometime later Rawlston returned home, fully laden from his shopping trip. He had counted the Arab's money and was now whistling to himself in his good fortune as he unloaded the legs of lamb and carried them into the house.

"You!"

The Sheikh's voice stopped him dead as his two henchmen came running. They grabbed hold of Rawlston and frogmarched him into the lounge, his parcels of meat dropping as they went.

"How much land do you own?"

"Me?"

"Bizmillah! Yes of course you! How much land do you own!"

"Why?"

Daggers appeared within his vision again.

"Well with the farms and the woods around the house here…"

"No, I am talking just of the fields at this time."

"Fields? Well, about six hundred acres."

"Acres? What is 'acres'? I am talking about the length of the fields out there!"

They frogmarched him to the window.

"There! From left to right is how much distance?"

"Er, just over a mile I suppose, I've never really measured it."

"You have a map?"

"Well I have a plan."

"Get it now!"

They released Rawlston and went with him into his study. He spread the plan on the table and explained the extent of the estate. He measured off the fields that the Sheikh had indicated and found them to be one and a quarter miles in length.

"Good! I will buy the fields!" said the Sheikh.

"But you can't! They're not for sale! Even if they were you would have to buy it all, the farm, the fishing, the woods, the house! But I'm telling you it's not for sale!"

"Silence! What is the price for everything?"

"Look, be reasonable! This is my home! I've been here twelve years! You don't understand! You can't just come barging in here and make me sell it to you! How would you like it?"

"You would buy my desert?"

They laughed.

The Sheikh came close to Rawlston and studied him.

"What is your name?"

"Rawlston. Geoffrey Rawlston."

"Mr.Rolton, it is you who does not understand. I wish to buy your home and you have already seen what I can pay for the things that I want. Now you have this chance to sell your home to me very well and you must think quickly of a price because I wish to purchase and I will not be denied! Do you understand?"

"Oh Christ! What the bloody hell is going on? I don't want to sell! I don't need to sell! This is unfair!"

"The price! I want to know the price!"

The only thing that Rawlston could do was to acquiesce to the Sheikh's demands and think quickly. He knew what the estate was worth, he looked at the daggers, it was all too much to deal with coming straight out of nowhere at him. He added a large amount to the estate's value.

"A million pounds!"

"One million pounds?"

"Er, yes, a million pounds, but if that's a bit high I could always…"

"Agreed! You arrange for the papers to sign and we shall pay you. Would you like to be paid in oil?"

"Oil?"

"It makes no difference. Whatever and however you wish to be paid it will be done. Oh, and do not cross me Mr.Rolton for we have a saying that a man's life, like water in our desert, is with us only briefly."

"Oh Christ!"

"So now you have your ladies cook our meal and we eat!"

Countdown

It had taken the Major four days in bed to get almost back to his old self.

Mrs.Ferzakerley's home cooking had done him the world of good and when he finally got dressed and went downstairs for the first time since his escapade at the river he had been astonished to find his cottage spick and span with not so much as a speck of dust in sight. He had worried about how much to pay her for all the work, but Mrs.Ferzakerley had simply said that if he could catch her a couple of salmon at some time then that would be payment enough and she insisted on looking in on him regularly in future. She also wanted him to go down to the butcher for his first walk to see the great fish, but the Major simply couldn't remember anything about any great fish, so Mrs.Ferzakerley got Sergeant Hughes to pay him a visit.

"How are you doing, Major?"

"Fine now, thanks Sergeant. I understand I've got you and Mrs.Ferzakerley to thank as well as my lucky stars for still being here."

"Don't you worry about that Major, for my part I was just doing my job. What I really want to hear is the story of the great fish."

"I'm sorry to say that the great fish is a great mystery Sergeant. I can't remember anything about any great fish. How big was it?"

"Forty four pounds on the butcher's scale."

"What! But that's incredible!"

"You broke the river record by a considerable distance. I shan't easily forget the sight of you and that fish lying there on the riverbank. Are you sure you can't remember anything?"

"Not a thing I'm afraid old boy."

The only thing he could remember was Rawlston's visit to the cottage and firing the revolver, which he was not about to disclose.

"It's very strange considering I used to have such a good memory, anyway I gather the fish is still at the butchers?"

"Yes and I've been thinking, you really ought to get it stuffed, set up I mean, there's a chap over at Balscombe who does a grand job and puts them in a glass case with gold lettering on the front. I've had a word with him and he'll reduce his price to a hundred and fifty pounds just so he can say he was the one who stuffed the record fish. What do you say?"

"A hundred and fifty pounds? It's a bit difficult really."

"Well everyone in the village is expecting you to put it on the wall in a glass case, so it's preserved for all time."

"Look Bert, can I talk to you in confidence?"

"Surely Major."

"You see it's the money. This is really very difficult. Things are not too good with my finances at this time and a hundred and fifty pounds is out of the question, even though I admit I'm being offered great value for money. Things are so tight I'm going to have to leave here at the end of the month as I can't afford to renew the lease, much to the delight of Rawlston. I've really got to save every penny I can to get myself into some sort of old people's home. I'm afraid I just can't afford to pay to have the fish set up, much as I'd like to have it done."

"Oh, dear me, I'm very sorry to hear things are that bad Major. I always thought you army officers had everything organised including your finances. Won't Rawlston give you some leeway and let you stay on?"

"Absolutely not, bloody man. No, I'm afraid that this it for me. Still I've had a good run you know, can't complain."

The Sergeant got up to leave.

"Showed the Jerries a thing or two I suppose?"

"Just a thing or two, Sergeant," said the Major as he showed the policeman out.

Bert Hughes was greatly concerned. It was such a miserable end to George Roberts' having lived for so long on the river he loved for Rawlston to be able to kick him out. He pondered the problem as he walked back to the village, crossed the green and entered the Flying Start. Mickey saw him coming and hailed him from behind the bar.

"Good day officer. What can we do for you this lunchtime? Large brandy is it?"

Bert smiled as everyone could see he was in uniform and obviously on duty.

"Less of your cheek landlord and anyway I'd want to know when your measures were last checked before I buy any shorts in here. No, I tell you what it is Mickey."

The sergeant surveyed the folk in the pub, finding them all to be locals.

"It's about the Major and his record fish."

"Oh?"

"Mind it's in confidence now, the old bugger would have me shot if he knew I was talking about this to anyone."

"Alright, in confidence then Bert."

"As it turns out the Major can't afford to have the fish stuffed. I got him a deal at a hundred and fifty quid and he can't afford it. Not only that but Rawlston's forcing him out of the cottage and he's going to have to leave at the end of the month and go into some kind of home."

"No, surely not, I thought you army types had all the money and it was just us poor workers that struggled?"

"Yes, well that's what I thought about officers, just shows how wrong you can be, doesn't it? As for us 'other ranks' we happen to struggle along just the same as everyone else for your information."

Mickey was thinking.

"We've got to get that fish set up for the Major so he can take it away with him Bert. We ought to have a whip round, you know, start a collection to stuff the fish. We should be able to get a hundred and fifty quid together from the village and if we happen to get more we'll give it to the Major to see him alright."

"So it's a myth you're just a hard hearted publican?"

"Very funny Bert."

"Can I leave it to you then?"

"Yes, I'll take care of it. Oh, by the way..."

He was holding his hand out towards the policeman.

"What?"

"How about a fiver, officer, just to start the ball rolling seeing as how you're so concerned?"

Bert looked around the bar at all the nodding faces and reached into his pocket.

"Oh alright then, I suppose I asked for it."

"Yes officer, that you certainly did."

Hetty Joy Verbeer was expertly conducting a fact finding mission as she reconnoitred the village.

She was adept at surreptitiously finding out all kinds of intimate facts about who was who, what was what, who controlled things, who ran things and who mattered in the machinations of village life. She made straight for the vicar, the largest local encyclopaedia, and gleaned information with every passing minute of the hour and a half she spent having tea in the vicarage. Then she went to the pub and talked on and off for a spell with Mrs.Mickey who was serving behind the bar, followed that by tracking down Mrs.Ferzakerley for another good gossip and ended the day by spending half an hour talking with Sergeant Hughes. She could remember every single fact she had learned without writing anything down and in the evening she exchanged information with her husband. Working steadily at it they built a precise picture of the way things were in the village.

The following morning the General knocked on the Major's door.

"Morning! You must be Major Roberts. The name's Chuck Verbeer, General Chuck Verbeer. I'm in town for this auction so seeing as how I heard so much about a famous fishing Major I thought I might pay you a little visit, if that's OK with you?"

George Roberts brightened hugely. He had been sitting in his den contemplating his future, reading a letter from a home for retired army officers. The prospect had been less than uplifting, but suddenly and unbelievably here was a real live American general standing on his doorstep.

"My dear fellow, do come in! How on earth did you happen to find me?"

"Hey everyone's talking about the Major and this great fish he caught, a salmon wasn't it?"

"Yes it was. Are you interested in fishing?"

"Don't really know much about it," said the General untruthfully, "but I sure would like to. Say, what kind of unit were you in Major?"

"Oh, tanks you know, and you?"

"Hey, tanks too! I was out in the Pacific for a while and then they put me over in Europe towards the end, Battle of the Bulge and on into Germany. How was it for you guys? See much action?"

"Some. North Africa actually, got wounded early on."

"Africa, so that would be the old Matildas?"

"Why yes, that's right."

The Major was surprised at the General's knowledge.

"With that useless three pound gun?"

"Two pounder actually, but you're right, it was pretty useless."

"So what happened after you were wounded?"

"POW, I think you can guess the rest."

"I'm sorry to hear that, but I see you made it through, guess we're the lucky ones."

"Yes, indeed we are. Want some tea?"

"Tea! English tea in England with an army buddy, what could be better?"

The Major showed the General around the cottage and they sat in his den with its photographs and fishing equipment. They drank tea and shared a biscuit or two and talked about the village, the army and the war. For a couple of hours George Roberts was taken away from his humble abode and his problems and transported around the world by their conversation. He came alive with the reminiscences and army stories. He liked this big, amiable American immensely and his respect for the man quickly built as time passed. He made a sandwich for their lunch and then asked the General if he would like to go fishing for an hour or two.

"Well I ain't going to do the fishing George, so I'll just watch, but I sure would like to see where you got the big fish."

They set off down to the Railway Pool talking as they made their way and stopping occasionally as the Major pointed out landmarks and places in the river where salmon could be caught. The General sat on the bank as the Major demonstrated how he fly fished the Railway Pool and for quarter of an hour George Roberts' great fly rod powered back and forth. He finished fishing, reeled in the line and hooked the fly to the rod's cork handle and as he did so a salmon rose out in the pool with a resounding splash, precisely where his fly had just been.

"Always the way," he said, smiling.

"You sure are good at this George."

"Practice old boy, practice. I've done it all my life so I should be good at it, shouldn't I? But it's easily taught you know."

"Have you taught people?"

"Yes I have and very satisfying it is too, imparting your knowledge to someone who is keen to learn. Lots of people find fishing very therapeutic because it takes their minds off things. I know I certainly find it so. By the way this is the spot where they found me with the big fish."

"Found you?"

"Yes, must have passed out or something. Funny thing is I can't remember a thing about catching it. Still they say it was me who caught it, so I suppose I must have."

They both laughed as they sat together on the riverbank.

"If you don't mind my asking George, what kind of things would you need your mind taking off? Surely you have no problems here?"

The Major sat looking at a shoal of minnows milling about in the turbulence created by the water swirling around his wader clad feet. A flight of Mallard passed them heading downstream in the sunlight and he watched them disappear around the bend below.

"It was just the war old boy, just the war."

"Bad, eh?"

The Major nodded as he gazed into the water and said under his breath,

"I just wish they'd lived."

The General waited.

"A lot?"

"Yes."

George Roberts drew in his breath and let it out in a loud sigh.

"The whole bloody lot of them."

They sat there quietly for a few minutes, the General had been through this countless times and knew to take things slowly.

"What happened George?"

"Oh, it all went wrong old boy, ran out of fuel, couldn't get away. Bloody logistics let us down. I made the decision to stand and fight and Jerry gave us a right pounding. Everyone died, everyone that is except me."

The General instantly grasped the whole story. He too was looking into the water as he spoke slowly and reassuringly.

"That sounds to me like the story of war from time immemorial my friend. The triumphs, the disasters, the mistakes, the defeats, the unfairness and the craziness of it all. It's just cold, callous, uncaring warfare, the darkest side of all, shattering lives and breaking spirits. I've asked myself the question 'why?' a million times and the answer that keeps coming back is 'that's just the way life is'. I know it isn't much, but it's the only answer I get. We gave our youth to the world to make it a better place and a lot of our friends and people we knew gave their lives. It wasn't anyone's fault except those who started it.

You know, you and me are very alike, like you I took responsibility and as I moved up through the ranks I had to make countless decisions along the way. Thankfully many of them were right, but some were wrong and men died because of them. Men died even when they were right. That is what war is George, an impossible answer to every decision you make, an impossible, unfair answer. You're screwed whatever you do."

Minutes passed before the Major spoke.

"But it was my decision to stop, my decision to stand and fight. I could have surrendered and they would have lived. They died because of me."

"Surrender? The British? Without engaging the enemy? Not in this world. No George, if you don't mind my saying so I think you're wrong. You've already told me that it was the fuel. What option did you have if you were out of fuel? Why, I'd have done exactly the same thing. It really wasn't down to you, it was down to the fuel. After all you weren't responsible for the fuel supplies were you?"

"No, no I wasn't."

More time passed and neither man spoke. Finally they both stood up and started to walk back.

"You know Chuck you could be right. Perhaps it wasn't all my fault. Maybe the problem really was down to the bloody logistics."

"Yes George, I believe it was," said the General,

"It was all down to the bloody logistics."

Charles felt that he and the secretary had done well.

Working evenings in his small flat they had just managed to keep pace with the demand for auction catalogues and during the days they had somehow assuaged the constant stream of questions that came at them over the telephone. The two thousand printed catalogues had all been sent out and they were now into the first of a thousand photocopies. Charles was relieved that the expensive colour inserts had all gone and were thankfully out of Shipley's sight.

The secretary had decided it would be better if she left her job too as she didn't want to catch the fallout from Shipley on her own, but not before having helped Charles complete the auction. Charles had then let her into the secrets of some more of the goings on that he and Nancy were stage-managing behind the scenes. She had immediately insisted that he should tell her no more so that she could always claim ignorance should Shipley ever question her.

For his part Shipley had noticed that the telephone in the front office seemed to be constantly ringing and that quite a lot of people might be coming to his auction, but he had yet to see a catalogue.

"Montgomery, where is my copy of the catalogue?"

"Er, well you'll have to have one of these photocopies Mr.Shipley."

"Photocopies! Why boy?"

"I didn't want to order too many catalogues this time sir, to save us expense, so as the printed ones have all gone out we're running on photocopies."

The secretary blushed.

"Hmm, let's see it then. Good, good. How many lots do we have in all?"

"Over two thousand, sir."

"Two thousand! Good Lord! I had no idea it was so much, why didn't you tell me?"

"You told me to get on with it and make this a stupendous auction Mr.Shipley, so I've been doing just that."

"But two thousand, that'll take days to get through. We'll have to cut it in half and sell the other half another time."

"Ooh, we couldn't possibly do that Mr.Shipley, I mean there are a lot of people coming a long way to this auction and they've expressed interest in all kinds of items from throughout the entire catalogue. Don't you think we could get into trouble if someone's come a great distance, say from Scotland, and then we're not selling the very items they've come to buy? We could lay ourselves open to all kinds of claims for costs, couldn't we?"

"But two thousand lots are going to take at least three days to sell. Anyway how could we possibly have enough people coming to guarantee our selling a large enough percentage of all these items?"

"Oh I think we're going to have an awful lot of people at this auction Mr.Shipley, I mean the phone never stops."

"How many do you think?"

"Well we've sent out, now let's see, yes, a hundred and fifty catalogues and then we've had more than another two hundred enquiries, so I suppose there could be up to four hundred people coming."

"Four hundred people! What on earth is going on? How could four hundred people even know about the auction?"

"Well it seems our adverts got picked up by some of the bigger newspapers. I remember answering some questions for a reporter some time ago and apparently there have been articles in some of the national papers about the auction. At least it means we'll have a chance of selling everything."

"Yes, I see, that's very good. But two thousand lots, four hundred people... Wait a minute! The hall only takes three hundred, what are we going to do with the others?"

Charles pondered a minute and waited for Shipley to come up with the answer.

He didn't, so Charles continued.

"Maybe..."

"Maybe what?"

"Maybe we could hold the auction in two venues at the same time?"

"Don't be ridiculous boy, we're not a major auction house taking bids over the telephone and all that nonsense."

"No sir, but maybe we ought to try it. We could use the marquee as the other venue and hire a public address system for you to talk to them on and then we could have someone in there taking bids and calling them back to us in the hall over a field telephone."

"Oh Lord, I usually have enough difficulty dealing with people in the hall. How can I be expected to cope with phone bidding as well over a three day sale?"

"I was just thinking of all the commission we'd be making. I mean if we could sell a large percentage of the lots it would be good money coming into the firm, wouldn't it, sir?"

Shipley looked at Charles, the secretary squirmed in her seat and greed won the day.

"I might have misjudged you just a little Montgomery. Can you put all this together properly by sale day?"

"Oh, yes sir, you just leave it to me Mr.Shipley and I'll put it together for you alright."

"Well you'll have to keep me in touch with developments and let me know about any bids that come in before the sale. Mark them all down properly in the sale book."

"Books, Mr.Shipley."

"Oh yes, of course, well get on with it and well done Montgomery, well done."

Shipley went off into his back office to telephone Rawlston and break the good news about how much money they were going to make from the auction.

Charles picked up the phone and dialled, as he waited for an answer he looked at the secretary, whose face was now bright pink, and smiled. He enquired of the voice on the other end of the line how much a full P.A. system would be to hire, set up and run to three or four different places with a field telephone in each and could they advise him where to hire mobile toilets.

The secretary began to cry again.

The black limousine swept into the farmyard.

The farmer came out of one of the buildings where he had been servicing a tractor and his wife came out of the house.

"Good morning! Good morning! I am pleased to meet you," said the Sheikh to the surprised couple.

"You are the good farmer of this land are you not?"

"Yes, I am. Twenty seven years we've been farming on the estate."

"Ah, the estate, ah, yes. I have reached an agreement with Mr.Rolton, you know him?"

"Mr.Rawlston? Yes, the estate owner, that's who we rent from."

"A difficult man," said the Sheikh to no one in particular.

The farmer looked at his wife, but they said nothing.

"I have come to an agreement with Mr.Rolton to buy the estate and then you would be working for me would you not?"

"Buy the estate? That is a surprise. I didn't know he was thinking of selling. Well, if you were to buy it we wouldn't exactly be working for you, but we would be paying you rent."

"Rent, yes, I see. Tell me," said the Sheikh walking towards the corner of the yard, "what do you know about animals?"

"Animals? Well, just about everything there is to know I suppose," said the farmer as they walked with him.

"Horses?"

"Ooh well, we haven't done horses in donkey's years, have we dear?" he asked his wife and they both started laughing.

"'Horses in donkey's years'. Yes! Very amusing!" said the Sheikh.

"But we rent the farm and so we rear what provides us with good income to pay the rent. You see, horses wouldn't provide us with enough income."

"Ah, but my horses will. For a start I intend to reduce your rent to, let us say...nothing...and then I intend to convert your farm buildings for my horses and I want you and your dear wife here to please help me with them."

"No rent! Well I never! Are you sure? But then how do we get our income?"

"You will get it from me. I will pay you to run my stables. I am not concerned about your knowledge of horses at this time for I have looked at the animals you have on your farm and you keep them well. We can increase your knowledge of horses as time goes on."

"Pay us? You mean we work for you?" the farmer was obviously concerned.

"Ah! Do not worry. You would keep the farmhouse as you have it now, so you have the right to stay here. But instead of depending on selling your animals to get your income I will simply pay you for running my stables. Then I am your market. No?"

"Yes, I see," said the farmer, although he wasn't quite sure that he did. They had reached the edge of the buildings. The fields opened out before them and in the distance the silvery river wended its way along the valley.

"These fields, how far do they go in that direction?"

"Right along to the copse by the bend in the river," said the farmer pointing.

"Copse? What is copse?"

"Oh, you see that small wood down there on the river bank, it might be a bit difficult at this distance, but just look to the bend in the river."

"Ah, yes, and who owns the fields past that?"

"Well they're for sale as you mention it. They're owned by Johnny Enright and they're getting on a bit are Johnny and Mrs.Enright so they've decided to sell."

"Really," said the Sheikh, his eyes twinkling.

"How much further would his fields go?"

"Must be another three quarters of a mile or so I would think."

The Sheikh nodded slowly.

"Tell me, you would be able to show from your books how much money you have made here per year, which you call your income, would you not?"

"Yes, yes I would."

"And these books would be correct?"

"Well... just about."

"So. As long as these accounts are honest I shall pay you double your best year out of the last ten years for every year that you work with me. You will help me, no?"

"Double!"

"Yes, double."

"Double! Yes of course I'll help you. Double! What exactly is it you want me to do?"

"The first thing I want you to do is to introduce me to this Mr.Endright. The second thing is to get rid of all your animals from the fields and the third thing is to think. I want you to think about taking away all the walls and fences from around the fields the moment I have bought from Mr.Rolton. There, right across the land I want everything removed and the land made so that my horses can run from that direction right across to the other side of the estate."

"You mean a gallop! That's what you want. A gallop!" said the farmer excitedly.

"Well, we could get the JCB going and take the walls down and the fences could come out easily enough. We could sell the stone from the walls and get some money back that way and then we could..."

"I can see you are a thinking man! This is good. Are you prepared to work with me and be my friends here in England?"

The farmer and his wife looked at each other.

"Yes, why yes, we are. But what exactly would you like us to call you?"

"My name is very difficult so what would you like to call me?" said the Sheikh.

The farmer thought for a minute.

"Would it be alright if we just called you 'Sheikh'?"

"Perfect. So now we go to Mr.Endright. No, wait, I am too fast as usual. Perhaps your good wife would give us some tea and then we go to Mr.Endright?"

"Give you a cup of tea? Of course we will."

The farmer and his wife and the Arabs began to walk back to the house. The Sheikh was pleased, the farmer was overwhelmed and his wife was beginning to panic at the thought of having to serve tea to an Arab Sheikh.

"You know that's exactly what the village was back in the olden days, don't you?" said the farmer as they came back into the yard.

"I am sorry? I do not understand."

"Well, a long, long time ago the village was the centre for all the horse drawn traffic travelling the valleys and was known for its blacksmith and saddlery. That's how it became called Little Saddlington they do say. 'Little Saddling Town' you see. There was a famous hunt that operated from here and the horses reared in this district were highly thought of and sought after. It all gradually died out with the age of the motor car and the breaking up of the land into smaller ownerships. Strange you should want to turn the clock back and bring horses back here again."

The Sheikh looked at the Religious One and they both looked at his son trying to catch a couple of elusive chickens at the other end of the yard.

"It is Allah's wish, my Lord," said the Religious One.

"Indeed," said the Sheikh and they called to the boy and together they went into the farmhouse to have tea.

Sergeant Hughes was having his own cup of tea when Charles entered the police station, in reality a room with a counter at the front of the policeman's house.

Bert Hughes knew Charles well and had often wondered how he kept his job working for Shipley, putting it down as a credit to the young man for sticking to the task and not walking out. It showed some character and Bert was big on character.

"Can I talk to you about a hypothetical situation, Sergeant?"

"Yes you certainly can," said Bert, knowing full well what that usually meant. "I deal with them all the time."

"Really?" Charles seemed relieved.

"Oh you wouldn't believe how many hypothetical situations come walking in here. Want a cup of tea?"

"Oh, yes, yes please, actually it's to do with a hypothetical auction house."

Bert turned back from making the tea.

"An auction house?"

"Yes, you know, a hypothetical one... of course."

Bert looked at him sternly.

"You know... a hypothetical one?" said Charles beginning to get hot under the collar.

The queue to get into the Flying Start spilled out onto the village green.

It was difficult to say whether this welcome increase in business was due to the wondrous new Australian barmaid or the number of people arriving daily in the village. With no one able to get easily in or out orders were passed forward to the bar, drinks were passed back, payment was passed forward and change was passed back again. Humour amongst the crowds was rife as everyone realised there was little point in complaining. The amount of beer and alcohol that was flowing out of the pub along with Mickey's intention to set up another bar near the marquee had resulted in a quadrupling of his orders. His plans for supplying food had sent his staff begging fridge and freezer space from friends as the pub's own became full. With storage arranged for countless loaves of bread, meats, salad, vegetables and all kinds of goodies they were ready to supply an army, which was exactly what they were going to have to do.

Then there were the sides of beef.

Bill Boyd had decided to go the whole hog and had convinced Mickey to order six whole beef carcasses, which he intended to spit roast out on the green, claiming that Australians could barbecue anything and pointing out they'd make good money from them. Bill had wanted to order ten but Mickey had not been too sure about the idea and ten seemed such a huge quantity. He'd finally managed to convince Bill that they should only order the six and even then they were going to cost enough. They had hired trestle tables and benches by the dozen and a humungous quantity of cutlery, plates and glasses. A strange kind of business relationship had sprung up between the two of them. Mickey had no idea how much he'd have to pay Bill for all the work he was doing, but things were running at such a pace he hardly had time to worry.

The name of the game was just to get everything done in time.

He could hardly believe his ears when the brewery, having looked at his increasing orders and heard about the amount of people in the area, asked him whether he would like a tanker load of beer. He readily accepted on condition that he only had to pay for the beer consumed.

"Quiet! Quiet! Listen everyone, I've got some important news!"

Everyone in the pub shouted at everyone else to be quiet so the noise became even louder. After a while it seemed to penetrate that everyone was to shut up so that Mickey could speak.

"Listen everyone, I've just made an agreement with the brewery that they're going to send us a tanker, a tanker load of beer!"

The roof of the pub nearly lifted off as a great cheer went up and spread outside onto the green.

Priorities, it would seem, had all been taken care of.

"Well, what do you think?"

Charles looked at the object.

"What is it?"

"Dunno. It's a family heirloom I brought over with me."

"But what is it?"

Bill Boyd sucked in his breath and shrugged.

"Dunno."

"What am I going to catalogue it as if I don't know what it is? Could it be some kind of line winder, like a bobbin type thing for a spinning wheel?"

"I suppose it could be, but why's it got that glass side and all those blued cogs and springs?"

It was Charles' turn to shrug.

"I wonder what that spike thing's for? Look at all that foliate engraving, it's really beautiful. I'll have to try and think of a description for it. Now then, we need to fill in an entry form and the charges are 10% of the sale price, two pounds handling charge and two pounds insurance, unless you want it insured for more than a hundred pounds in which case the premium increases. And of course it all has 14% VAT on top."

"Wait a minute! I don't want to pay all that to your lot. What about my costs of getting here?"

"I'm sorry but our charges are standard for whatever the item is or however it's transported to us. If you had a lot of items to sell or something really valuable I could lower our commission a bit, but for this?"

He looked at the object sitting on the table in all of its fine and unknown splendour.

"OK let's forget about the auction proper, how about my holding a little private auction? You could show this to a few people and tell 'em to come to the pub at a certain time if they're interested and I could auction it to the highest bidder!"

"Mr.Boyd! I'd get shot! Anyway you'll have Mr.Shipley after you if you try to take advantage of our costs in getting all these people to come here."

"Who the hell's Shipley?"

"The auctioneer."

"Oh, to hell with him, I just want to sell me heirloom. Now then, tell me more about this public address system you're installing, sounds like a bit of a good thing to me..."

Bert Hughes was walking towards the Major.

"Bit of a big marquee, Major."

"Indeed, what exactly is it for?"

"Eric Shipley's auction which I gather is going to be rather large seeing the amount of people about."

"I hope the weather stays fine for it. When does it start?"

"Viewing starts on Thursday, they've had to extend it because of all the interest. The actual auction will start the following Monday and probably run until the Thursday night. I must say it's going to be a big affair, the village will be packed with people. You don't fancy a lunchtime half pint by any chance to you?"

"A half pint? Well, I suppose it wouldn't do me any harm, would it? But you're in uniform."

"Don't worry about that Major, no one'll tell."

They walked towards the pub with Bert more than happy that the local grapevine had correctly advised him of George Roberts' whereabouts and that everything was hopefully going to work out the way it had been planned. As they approached the pub he saw a curtain move and trusted that those inside were ready.

"After you Major."

As the Major opened the door and walked in a voice called out,

"Three cheers for the Major! Hip-hip!"

There came a resounding 'Hooray!'

"Hip-Hip!"

"Hooray!"

"Hip-Hip!"

"Hooray!" they shouted and burst into applause.

George Roberts stood there in astonishment.

"Come in Major, I've taken the liberty of pouring you a pint of your favourite," said Mickey.

The Major and the Sergeant approached the bar and both looked at the gorgeous, smiling and well endowed new barmaid standing at Mickey's elbow.

"Now then Major, don't look so surprised to see all your friends gathered around you because we're here for a special occasion that we hope you'll be pleased with. A little while ago, when you were found on the riverbank, you had us all worried that you might not be going to be with us much longer. To our relief that scare proved groundless, but now we gather you really are going to have to leave us and so, being the conniving bunch that we are," a laugh went around the bar, "we decided not to let you go without knowing how much we've enjoyed you being in our midst for all these years. It's not often you find someone that nobody has a bad word for. Well one man does, but he don't count."

A murmur of something that sounded like 'No, he bloody doesn't!' passed around the company.

"Someone that all of us have been delighted to know as a friend and a gentleman, someone who has shown the way to many of us in the art of fishing for the wily salmon."

He glanced at Dirk and Terry and a more knowing laugh ensued.

"So we've done something on which all of us were unanimously agreed and if you'll just step over to that table Dirk and Terry have something to show you."

Completely mystified the Major did as he was asked and found himself looking at a very large object covered by a sheet. Dirk and Terry stood to either side of it and together they removed the sheet exposing the stuffed 44lb. salmon superbly set up in a bow fronted glass case. The huge fish was mounted swimming over a rocky river bed and looked simply magnificent, the size of its girth was formidable with the mother of pearl sheen on its flanks giving it such a lifelike appearance. The gold lettering on the bowed glass front read:

'Record 44lb. Salmon caught on Fly by Major George Roberts in the Railway Pool 26/4/79'.

The Major was speechless as he looked at what was by far the largest salmon of his life and was more baffled than ever by his inability to recall their previous meeting.

"Well what do you think?" asked Bert Hughes.

"We'd all like to hear the story of the fight Major, but we realise we may never get to do so," said Mickey.

"No, but I promise you this."

The Major turned to his friends.

"If I ever do remember you'll all be the first to hear about it. But I am embarrassed you know as to how this came to be paid for."

"Ah, well Major," said Mickey, "we decided that seeing as you weren't so well we'd have a whip round and everyone contributed so it's all fully paid for. In fact we raised seventy two pounds more than was needed, which we think you should have, just to tide you over 'til you get settled wherever it is you're going."

The Major was overcome and quickly reached into his pocket to dab away a tear that threatened to spill from his eye.

Now everyone was embarrassed.

"Well I think I need a drink after that, thank you all. I'm really very grateful to each and every one of you."

Relieved they applauded again as the Major walked to the bar, picked up his pint and raised it to them. They drank his health and began admiring the fish again. As the noise increased Terry said quietly to the Major,

"Must have been one that slipped past us, eh, Major?"

"MTM here!"

The secretary nearly jumped out of her skin at the sharp voice. A stout, balding man wearing a blue boiler suit was standing in the doorway to the office.

"You frightened the living daylights out of me!" she exclaimed.

"Sorry about that, but I was told to get here as quick as I could."

"Who did you say you were from?"

"No, it's me, MTM," said the man.

"I don't understand, have you some business at the auction?"

"I sincerely hope so, otherwise this lot are going to be in trouble aren't they?" he pointed out of the front door of the hall at the people in the square.

"I'm sorry?"

"It's me. MTM."

The secretary thought she should get Mr.Montgomery and called him over from the stage.

"Are you Montgomery?" asked the man.

57

"Yes, I am, what can I do for you?"

"I'm MTM. You know, you asked me to come and help out."

"MTM? I don't really follow."

The man undid some buttons on his boiler suit and pulled it apart to display a printed T-shirt beneath.

"That's me. MTM," he said, grinning at them.

The T-shirt read 'Mobile Toilet Man' above a picture of a toilet on wheels travelling at great speed.

"There's Superman and then there's me, Mobile Toilet Man. Want a T-shirt?"

Charles and the secretary looked at each other.

The man was obviously a bit crackers.

"No thanks, so you've arrived, that's good." said Charles.

"Never let it be said that Mobile Toilet Man ever let anyone down. He flies through the skies doing good where he can and goes through all the motions. 'Motions', get it?"

Charles and the secretary looked at each other.

"Whenever people are desperate they look to Mobile Toilet Man to help them and after he has they cry, 'Phew, that's a relief!'.

He burst into laughter.

"Very funny, now, have you got everything under control?"

"I have, but have they?" he said and pointed out of the front door again as he continued to chuckle.

"I mean the toilets, do you want to know where to put them?"

"Underneath people?"

"Look be serious will you?"

"OK, how about on the green?"

"Yes, that'll be fine, just keep them out of the way."

"Surely, out of sight out of mind, eh?"

"Something like that, yes."

"Fifty percent please."

"What?"

"Fifty percent up front or I can't deploy them and this lot'll go hopping mad. Fifty percent covers me."

"Alright, alright, fifty percent."

Charles filled out a cheque and duly handed it over.

"Hope this doesn't bounce or I'll have to empty the units on your green."

"It won't bounce, now kindly go off and do your work, would you?" said Charles, relieved as the man left them.

"What a nutter."

"I know Mr.Montgomery, he frightened the living daylights out of me earlier."

"Hey!"

They both jumped.

"It's a dirty job, but someone's got to do it!" shouted Mobile Toilet Man from the doorway and vanished.

The Viewing Days

It was now only seven days before the auction.

Shipley had moved the start of the viewing days of the items that were for sale even further forward due to the excessive amounts of people that had appeared in the village. For three days Rubicon and Shipley's removal van had been transporting numerous loads of sale goods between the hall and the marquee and they were all now exhibited by their numeric lot numbers in both locations ready for people to inspect. Charles had anticipated the amount of people who would be present and had employed a security guard with a dog to protect the goods in the marquee each night and another to watch out for any would-be thieves through the days.

Little Saddlington had turned into Big Saddlington.

More than a hundred caravans were dotted around the village outskirts along with some three hundred tents. The first traffic jams in the village's history were occurring as the hundreds of people staying in the surrounding area tried to get in to view the auction items. Every hotel within a thirty mile radius had laid on buses for their guests, but there was practically nowhere for them to park and along with all the other vehicles that were trying to get into the village chaos ensued.

In the middle of the melee Chuck Verbeeer ran into the police sergeant who was trying to sort out the worst of the jam.

"What you need is a little military organisation!" he yelled above the hooting car horns.

"You're right, I certainly could do with reinforcements! Unfortunately I'm on my own!" shouted Bert Hughes as he tried to direct the vehicles.

"Let's see if we can't make some sense of this mess!" said the General and the two of them began trying to sort out the snarl up.

They had only been at it for about fifteen minutes and were actually beginning to get somewhere when the traffic suddenly ground to a complete halt as a large number of ducks came waddling slowly across the road from the direction of the river, on their way to lunch.

The General and the policeman stood there bemused as, in a perfect line all evenly spaced and trailing one behind the other, the ducks took their own sweet time crossing the road. The two men smiled at each other and shook their heads as more ducks kept coming, waddling along completely unconcerned about the traffic chaos that was building up all around them.

'Smarten up there,' thought the General to himself as they paraded past him.

'You man, yes you, pick your feet up and you, stand up straight and at least look as if you're proud of yourself. Good, good, well done men, well done. Carry on,' he was having great trouble resisting a most dreadful urge when the policeman swept all resistance away.

"Do you think we should salute?"

'Oh hell,' thought the General, 'nobody knows me here.'

He nodded at the policeman and to the delight of the dozens of motorists hemmed in all around them they both saluted the Little Saddlington Duck

Contingent as it quietly waddled its way past them and off towards the square, leaving them with such an awful traffic problem that it took another half hour to get some semblance of a proper flow going again.

"You know you said reinforcements, Sergeant?"

"Yes."

"Well I seriously think you're going to need some otherwise this could turn into the greatest English log jam of all time."

"You're right, I'm certainly going to have to do something about it."

"Chuck Verbeer," the General held out his hand.

"Bert Hughes, thanks for the help, General. Oh, don't worry, Mrs.Verbeer told me all about you. Anyway it's my business to know who's who around here. I'll never keep track of this lot though. No madam, you cannot park there, now kindly move on!"

They began to make their way through the crowds to the police station where Bert rang up his headquarters and requested that six men be sent to Little Saddlington until the auction was over, but the best headquarters could do was to provide two and those for only three of the auction viewing days. Chuck Verbeer asked if he could try and arrange something and dialled a number from his address book

"Hello, can I speak to the base Commander? This is General Chuck Verbeer out of Reno, Nevada. My unit? Well just mention the word 'LAOS' to him would you? Yes, that's right. Yes, I'll hold."

"Base Commander?" enquired Bert Hughes.

The General winked.

"Hello, is that the base Commander? Good, this is General Chuck Verbeer, I gather you know about 'LAOS'? You are? Well, good to have you on board! Commander I'm over here in Little Saddlington. You haven't? Well I'm not surprised, it's a pretty small place, but we've got a traffic problem here that needs handling. It could go on for about...two weeks?"

Bert nodded.

"Now I now it's an unusual request but in terms of Anglo-American relations this could be a big one. I mean we've got traffic here like downtown New York, kind of limited parking, no one to control things... Ah-ha. Ah-ha...Yes, I see, well if you're happy to do that Commander that would be just fine, we'll expect them as soon as you can... Oh, good, good! Now if you're ever in Reno you'd be most welcome. OK, thank you Commander."

He put the phone down and looked at Bert Hughes.

"Well help is on its way, they aren't exactly the US cavalry but they'll handle this job real well."

"So who are they sending us?"

"Military Police. They're going to let us have fifteen Military Police."

"MP's? Good! That should sort this lot out."

"Yep, nothing will sort this lot out like American Military Police, they're a touch bunch and this particular group are tougher than most."

The General grinned.

"Oh?"

"You better believe it, they're women!"

Bob and Herpes entered the auctioneer's front office.

"I was wondering about your auction."

"Oh yes Bob?"

"Well I mean, how are you going to sort out who gets to sit here in the village hall?"

Charles was completely floored.

"Do you know I hadn't thought about that, it's a good point."

Bob's eyes gleamed.

"Well unless you want a free-for-all when you open up you better start selling tickets."

"Tickets?"

"Tickets."

Bob waited as the wheels within Charles' grey matter slowly turned.

"I've thought about it and I reckon it would be simple. If I got some raffle tickets and stuck one part to each seat then all that people would have to do would be to match up the counterpart to their seat. I could use different colours for different parts of the hall so people could find their seats easily."

"Yes. What's this 'I' business?"

"It's only that I'd thought about it and you obviously hadn't and maybe I could handle selling the tickets for you and save you a lot of work."

"Selling the tickets?"

"I reckon we can charge a fiver a seat a day and you've got three hundred and eleven seats in here..."

"Have we?"

Charles looked at the secretary.

"Counted 'em myself, that makes fifteen hundred and fifty five pounds a day you could be making. Sounds like an awful lot of money to me."

He eyed Charles warily.

"And you want to set this up and do the selling for a commission I suppose?"

"Well it's just that I'd thought about it and you hadn't and a bit of cash would come in handy like."

"What about Shipley?"

"What about Shipley? I won't tell him if you won't and by the time the auction starts and he realises what's going on it'll be too late for him to do anything about it."

"A fiver sounds like a lot to me Bob, maybe we should make it two pounds fifty?"

"No, stick to a fiver a seat. You don't want any old riff-raff inside the hall do you? What you want in the hall are the folks with the money and they're the ones who will be prepared to pay a bit to get a ringside seat so to speak. With all these people coming to the auction we'd be bound to sell out."

"We?"

"Well I'm presuming you'd be taking a commission as well, wouldn't you? I mean Shipley's not going to get anything out of it, is he?"

Charles was very conscious of the secretary's presence.

"Bob, I'd get the sack for doing that kind of thing as you well know."

"Don't know why you work in this place lad, you're wasted here and so are you lass."

He looked at the secretary, the secretary looked at Charles, Charles pondered, Bob waited, then seized the initiative.

"How's about a sixty-forty split then? Sixty for you two and forty for me?"

The secretary could not believe what she was hearing.

"You mean we get thirty percent each and you get forty percent?"

"Well I'd be doing all the work selling the tickets. It only seems fair to me."

"What do you think?" Charles asked the secretary who had already done the figures in her head, she nodded vigorously in agreement.

"Mind you Bob, we'd have to keep it from Shipley."

"Right you are, so that's it then, is it? We've got a deal?"

"I guess so, just make sure you don't cock it up for us will you?"

"Me? Cock it up? Never!"

But Charles wasn't going to trust to fate when it came to Bob's ability to handle things properly.

"I'll tell Shipley the tickets are free and you'll be on your own if he finds out."

"Alright Charles, I'll set the terrifying 'Erp on him if he starts anything, you just leave it to me."

Bill Boyd was waiting for Bob and Herpes out on the village green by the beer tanker.

"Did he go for it?"

"Yes, it's all agreed. A fiver a ticket."

"Five pounds each, that's good going mate."

"Brilliant idea of yours Bill, this cash is going to change my life. Are you sure you don't want anything out of it? I mean it's a lot of money."

"Nah, from what I can see your need is greater than mine, anyway you'll be buying me a drink or two, won't you?"

"At five pounds a ticket you bet I will."

However Bob's brain was already teasing with the idea that maybe he could charge more than a fiver a ticket and make a bit extra for himself on the side.

In fact maybe he could charge a lot more…

Just then a strange sound could be heard and people stopped talking to hear it better. It was strange but familiar at the same time and, as it grew in volume, everyone looked towards the village square as three Scottish bagpipers, dressed in full Highland regalia came marching around the corner of the hall.

Willie, Hamish and Rory Laird made a splendid picture. They marched once around the square and proceeded out onto the village green. People clapped in time to 'Scotland the Brave' as it sang from their bagpipes. The General stood listening, the sound of the pipes had always made him emotional, reminding him of the time the Brits fighting alongside him had launched an attack with bagpipes wailing as mortar shells exploded around them. A lump rose in his throat as the three Scots marched up and down the green and finally came to a halt, ceasing their playing in front of the beer tanker.

"I'm Willie Laird and these are my sons Hamish and Rory! We're here to give you English a sound beating in the auction room!" announced the Laird of the Highlands.

"How about us Australians mate?" enquired Bill Boyd.

"Australians don't count!" pronounced the Laird.

"Oh yes they do! Listen! One, two, three, four, five, six, seven, eight, nine, ten. There you are!"

"Och, you know what I mean laddie!"

"Yeah, I think so, want a beer lads?"

Willie Laird and his sons had arrived and created quite a stir with the pipes, although Willie had been concerned to see the amount of people gathered in the village and wondered whether that meant he would have a real fight on his hands to buy anything in the auction.

Try as he might Julius Polperro had not been able to find a single artefact in either the catalogue descriptions or the late entry sheets, but they had definitely been mentioned in the advertisement and he was eager to locate them. He had a ready market in the antiques trade for any kind of artefact and knew he could make a good turn on them. Frustrated at not having located any after searching through the vast amount of goods on view in the hall and the marquee he knocked on the door of the front office.

"Yes, sir, can I help you?" said Charles.

"I hope so, I simply can't find some of the things that were in your advertisement for the auction."

"Right, sir, what exactly was it that you were interested in?"

"Artefacts."

"Artefacts?"

"Artefacts."

"Oh, yes, artefacts."

Charles had known there would be a comeback to deal with over the descriptions he had put in the advertisements and hoped that people were not going to get too upset, especially if they had come a long distance.

"I think I know what it is you're after, sir, if you'll just follow me I'm sure I can locate it for you."

Julius cheered up at this and followed Charles out of the office.

"Have you come a long way?"

"Yes, from Cornwall."

"Ah, Cornwall, yes, I see."

They walked up the wooden steps at the side of the stage and Charles looked through his catalogue and searched amongst the items laid out on the tables.

"Here we are, sir, lot number eleven hundred and sixty two."

He turned to Julius and showed him the book he had picked up from the table.

"But that's not an artefact," said Julius and he was quite right.

"Well it does plainly say it is in the title, sir."

Julius looked at the cover of the book.

"You must be bloody joking!"

Charles had to keep a lid on things.

"No, sir. Why? Is there something wrong?"

"Wrong! Exactly what colour of canary do you take me for?"

"Canary, sir?"

"Listen to me you young smart aleck, I've been going to auctions for over thirty years and for you to describe this in your advertising as 'Artefacts' is a downright liberty! What a con! You've just used that word to get people like me to come all the way here in the hope that we'll buy something! 'Artefacts' my eye!"

"I'm not sure I follow you, sir. The book title is quite clear and correctly described in the catalogue, look."

"Never mind that," snapped Julius, "What about this?"

From his pocket he took a cutting of Rubicon & Shipley's advertisement.

"Do you see what it clearly states right there? Artefacts. Spelled A-R-T-E-F-A-C-T-S. What you're holding is not 'Artefacts', as if you didn't flaming well know!"

He was doing his best to try and stay annoyed, but couldn't help seeing the funny side of what the auction house had been up to.

"Ah well you see, sir, I think I know what happened, there must have been a typographical error."

Julius began shaking his head and laughed.

"Typographical error? Don't give me that load of old balls. 'Typographical error' my arse."

"Please sir, your language, there are ladies around."

"Oh are there? Sure they're not just more 'typographical errors'? How many people have you had to explain this to before me?"

Charles could see that the man was thankfully not too upset and confided in him.

"Well one or two actually."

"I'll bet you have, more like a few hundred I should think. Who had the brass neck to pull a stunt like this? Was it you?"

"No, it's not a stunt sir, as I told you it's just a…"

"'Typographical bloody error', yes, I know that's what you said, I just don't believe you."

At that moment a small, white haired, elderly man interrupted them and enquired of Charles where the artefacts might be.

"Here," said Julius as he took the book from Charles and thrust it into the man's hands.

"What's this?"

"A typographical sodding error," replied Julius, laughing.

"I'm sorry I don't understand," said the man.

"You will if you read the title."

The man peered through the lower half of his gold rimmed bi-focals and read the title out loud.

"'Arty Facts. A reference work by Anne Richardson.' Is this some sort of joke?"

"I think you might be right, I was just saying to this smart aleck here that someone from the auctioneers is really trying our patience with this."

"But I don't understand, it clearly stated in the auction advertising that there were 'artefacts' for sale."

Julius turned and walked away, laughing to himself as he heard Charles begin explaining again.

"Well you see, sir, there seems to have been what we in the business call a 'typographical...'"

"Auction tickets for the village hall! Reserve your seats now!"

Bob raised his voice as he wandered about the village green.

"We can reserve our seats?"

"Yes sir, tickets are for sale for each day and different colours denote different parts of the hall. Blue is at the front, green is in the middle and yellow is at the back. Ten Pounds a ticket to get yourself a seat."

"Ten Pounds! What, even for those at the back?"

"That's right squire, they're the same price wherever you sit."

"That's outrageous! I'm not paying that each day!"

"Suit yourself, but if I were you I'd spend the money and get the best crack at the auctioneer, otherwise you mightn't buy anything."

"I'd like some tickets please, I want four for each of the first two days, would you take a cheque?" asked a woman.

"Not likely luv, cash only I'm afraid, if you haven't got it on you I can hold the tickets until you get it."

But she did have the cash and so Bob supplied the tickets and pocketed the money.

"Oh alright then, but this is daylight robbery."

"Yes, I know it is, guvnor."

"Two tickets for four days then and I want blue ones, I want to be right up at the front for that price."

"Right you are squire."

And so Bob sold the tickets for the seating in the village hall. He gave a few out to his friends free of charge, but most were sold to the throng in and around the village. He made two trips to increase sales, one to the Tudor Arms and one to the Somerville Hotel where the patrons just about cleaned him out. Each day he came back to the pub laden with cash and he and Bill Boyd sorted it out, but not before Bob had already stashed approximately half of his takings at home. They divided up the money and each morning Bob would pass by the office with two brown envelopes for Charles and the secretary.

Neither of them had any idea he was charging double the agreed amount, but sooner or later Bob was going to find it very hard to cover up his deceit.

The fifteen female American Military Police arrived early in the morning on the second day of the auction viewing. They rolled up to the police station in three huge army trucks and reported to the General and Sergeant Hughes. Unlike the General the Sergeant was amazed to find that they didn't need accommodation or food, nor did they require much instruction on how to deal with the traffic problem. The General stood with the Lieutenant in charge and together they rapidly worked out the best approach. It seemed they hadn't been there minutes when the Lieutenant saluted the General, climbed into the front of the first truck and off they drove.

"Where are they going to sleep?" Bert asked.

"Oh, don't worry about them, they'll be fully organised and on duty in a short while. Then you can sit back and put your feet up."

"Oh yes? You think this lot'll run sweetly then?"

"I was just kidding, but you can forget the traffic problem anyway, it's all under control now. I just hope they remember that it's civilians they're dealing with out there."

The trucks crossed the bridge and made their way out of the village. Stopping after half a mile they turned into a secluded field, sheltered by trees on both sides. For the next hour the fifteen women set up a camp the General would have been proud of. Tents, hammocks, sleeping bags, kitchens, latrines, showers, communications, medical facilities and stores appeared as if by magic. When the first contingent left for traffic control duty they had breakfasted superbly and were more than ready for a 'no nonsense' day.

The first priority was to completely stop all traffic from entering the village by erecting two barriers at either end of the main street, one of them on the other side of the bridge in the direction of the MP's camp, and a third along the minor road into the village.

Too bad if you were trying to drive through Little Saddlington because from the moment they went on duty everyone was stopped and turned around at the barriers unless their names were on a fairly extensive list that Bert Hughes had drawn up. Those on the list were either concerned with working in Little Saddlington or were locals or landed gentry. Apart from them no one was getting in with a vehicle. At each of the two main barriers there was a designated turning area for buses, none of which were allowed to disembark their passengers until fully turned around and pointed in the opposite direction.

Driver's complaints fell on deaf ears and whether they liked it or not they had to drive back the way they had come and find somewhere else to park.

On that first day there were arguments a many, but the MP's set the precedent and those who had their vehicles turned back were given due warning that this was how it was going to be for the duration of the auction.

The main road along the valley became a solid line of parked cars down either side, leaving barely enough room for two vehicles to pass each other.

Exasperated drivers approached local farmers with financial offers and soon empty fields were being opened up as car parks. The ingenuity of those desperate to park their vehicles knew no bounds and before long the Valley School had rows of vehicles stretching across its playing fields. By auction time itself all the taxi and mini-bus services for miles around would be fully booked and each day would drop their charges at the village barriers, picking them up later at prearranged times. Within twenty four hours, after having to add a few more names to the list of those who were allowed into the village, the traffic problem came fully under control.

It took only nine of the MP's to run the three barriers allowing a reasonable duty roster to be set up. Once their period of duty ended they were able to go back to the camp to shower and get some rest, but instead they immediately headed straight for either the beer tanker or the Flying Start, where soon everyone got to know them pretty well.

These military women brought an air of organisation to the chaos that had descended upon Little Saddlington. Maybe it was their uniforms or just the way they went about things, but even through their simply wandering about the green people gained a sense of there being some firm protection present and consequently those who were thinking of misbehaving, in no matter how small a way, thought better of it. Everyone agreed they were a pretty good influence.

For their part the MP's rapidly identified all the available single men in the village, who soon found themselves being chatted up. Dirk and Terry were prime targets, but Bob came in for quite a bit of attention and even Herpes got his share.

On their second night, after the traffic had disappeared, twelve of the fifteen were in the pub whilst the other three were preparing dinner back at the camp. A tall Texan lady called Sally, or LT for short (Long Tall) was leaning on Terry's shoulder, Bob was showing Gail and Sue how to play darts and Dirk had Dolores, Rose and Dip (Serendipity) laughing with stories about the village.

Despite the attraction of the opposite sex Dirk and Terry could see the river mist forming. Neither were earning money from the auction opportunities and they were keen to take up their stations under the bridge. Their excuses for having to leave started early and escalated through the evening, but the women were not going to let them get away easily. Eventually the two of them went through to the toilets and slipped out of the pub the back way. Walking around to the front they were happy to see thick mist hanging directly over the river, but not so happy when they heard a voice they instantly recognised.

"And where might you pair of scoundrels be off to then?"

"Oh, good evening Sergeant Hughes, well we're just off home actually."

"Home? Home at nine o'clock? No lad, you two are certainly not off home, my guess is you're off to do a bit of salmon poaching in the mist. Now where would you be going to do that, I wonder?"

"No, not poaching Bert, not us, not anymore, you know that. We're just going home like good little boys."

"Good little boys my…"

The front door of the pub opened and LT, Sue and Dip came out.

"So here you two are, what seems to be the trouble officer?"

"Oh it's no trouble really miss, just this pair of scallywags getting up to no good as usual."

"And what kind of 'no good' would that be?"

"No, we aren't LT, honest, we're just going home like we told you."

The other MP's came out of the pub and gathered around them.

"Grown lads going home at nine o'clock? I think not. Ladies you are looking at the two most infamous poachers in this part of the world. This pair are capable of sneaking a pheasant or a hare or a salmon in the blink of an eye and it's my guess that's just what they were about to go and do."

"Poachers?" said LT, "Well we can't have that going on, now can we Sergeant Hughes?"

"No miss, it's a very bad thing is poaching, stealing it is really and we don't much like having thieves in our village."

"What's going on 'ere? In trouble, Terry?"

Bob had been upset at having lost the first female attention he'd enjoyed in a very long time and had followed them out. All twelve of the MP's had now surrounded the three men and not even Herpes could get through to his master.

"No, no trouble, it's just that Bert's gone bleedin' mad, thinks we're going poaching."

"Well, like I said, we can't have any of that going on while we're here, so what shall we do with them ladies?"

LT looked at the police Sergeant as, on Dolores' command, the others grabbed hold of the three men.

"So I guess we better take care of them tonight then, officer?" asked Sue as the men struggled to get free.

"Not my place to say miss, I think I'll ask the General… tomorrow."

"You do that Sergeant, you do that."

"Oi! Get off! What are you doing? Let go of me!"

But nothing was going to stop the women now and the three were briskly womanhandled across the road to the truck.

"Bert! Don't leave us Bert!" yelled Dirk.

Bert Hughes had no intention of being subjected to the same fate, whatever that might be going to be, so his helping the hapless three was out of the question. He just watched the proceedings with great amusement.

"What are you doing? I'm not a poacher!" complained Bob as he was slung unceremoniously up and onto the truck's hard floor.

"You might as well be because you're coming with us!"

"Wait a minute! Stop! What about the 'Erp?"

"'Erp! Get up there!" commanded Dolores.

Now Herpes admittedly was a bit daft, but he wasn't downright stupid and knew that tone of voice meant serious business. In one bound he leapt into the back of the truck and landed on top of his master.

"You turncoat!" shouted Bob as Dirk and Terry kept shouting for the women to stop. The truck started up and made for the bridge. Inside it female hands were undoing the men's shirts and trousers, despite their attempts at defending themselves.

"So why do you call him the 'Erp?" asked Dip.

"Because that's his bloody name! Herpes! He's got bloody Herpes!" yelled Terry, desperately trying to put the women off.

"Yeah, just like his master!" screamed Bob. For a few seconds the men thought they'd succeeded and that the American women were going to stop molesting them.

"Hell, we've all got worse than that!" said Dolores and the de-clothing resumed, accompanied by male screams of complaint as the truck crossed the bridge, leaving Bert Hughes chuckling to himself as he listened to their dwindling shouts for help.

The Laird of the Highlands located the two locked boxes at the same time as Julius Polperro. They looked them over, trying not to seem too interested, each being highly suspicious of the other.

"Have you heard of anything like this before?" asked Julius.

"Not me. Only the Sassenachs could lock something in a box and try to sell it in an auction."

"I don't believe the description: 'A Shagreen covered silver bound locked box thought to possibly contain jewellery and precious metal.' How on earth can they claim that?"

"Och, the English will say anything to make a sale. But there's definitely something in this one."

Willie had turned the box upside down and was shaking it.

"Less of that about the English, Jock, I'm a Cornishman and proud of it."

"Only joking ye ken, only joking, now then, what exactly is 'Shagreen'?"

"Shark skin," said Julius, impressed by the exterior of the boxes.

"Very appropriate seeing we're South of the Border. Ye dinna know what a 'jewellery' or a 'precious metal' sound might be like do ye, laddie?"

Julius decided he was not going to help the Scotsman by shaking the other box, so Willie picked it up and did so.

"Well something's rattling around in this one, no sense in getting worked up about them though because ye can't risk throwing money away on something that might be worthless, now can ye?"

"No, you can't. What do you intend doing about them?"

"I was just thinking of asking ye the same thing."

"I asked first."

"So ye did, laddie, so ye did."

Julius had taken an instant dislike to Willie, who he thought might be acting dumb to cover the fact that he really knew what the boxes contained. Willie Laird was thinking exactly the same thing about Julius and the two of them were re-enacting what had already taken place between quite a number of people over the two locked boxes and their mysterious contents.

That evening Shipley and Rawlston were congratulating each other over a drink at Rawlston Manor. Both of them were excited at the prospect of making many thousands of pounds from the auction now that there was such huge interest in it and Shipley was congratulating Rawlston on the forthcoming outrageously priced sale of his estate to the Sheikh. Looking through the photocopied catalogue at those items marked off as being theirs Rawlston observed that perhaps they should have entered more if the auction was going to be so well attended. Shipley suggested that if they used the late entry arrangements they could probably squeeze another hundred lots in.

In their greed they started taking things from the manor to sell.

When Rawlston had originally bought the estate the manor house had been full of paintings, antiques and furnishings. Some of these he had sold off whenever Shipley had been able to get him high prices for them and now that he was going to sell to the Sheikh he intended to take full advantage of this last opportunity.

He began laying his hands on a variety of items for Shipley to sell and piled them in the hall. Shipley wrote down the descriptions along with a ridiculously high guide price and gave them each a lot number. The reserve prices that Rawlston placed on them, the minimum they could be sold for, were extremely high for if they were not reached he would be quite happy to have them back. Not long after they had finished, leaving the pile of goods to await collection, the Arabs returned.

The Sheikh looked at everything in the hallway and Shipley and Rawlston explained that it was all going to be put into the auction.

"Now then, what couldn't you wallahs do with these?" asked Rawlston as he picked up an old sword and drew it halfway out of its scabbard.

"Japanese you know, probably belonged to an Emperor or something and doubtless worth thousands. You'll find several of them, they were in the house long before I bought it and they're all for sale."

The Arabs examined the swords.

"How much do you want for these Mr.Rolton?"

"Rawlston, Sheikh, my name is Rawlston."

"That is what I said Mr.Rolton. How much?"

"Oh you can't buy them now Sheikh. Oh, no. They have to go into the auction."

He looked at Shipley.

"Yes, they'll all be in one lot, you know, all together so you can buy them all at once."

"Then you will let me know when you are selling them. And do not forget."

With that they went upstairs to bed leaving Shipley and Rawlston to enjoy another hour of mutual congratulation over the prospect of driving up the price of the swords with non-existent mystery bids the moment the Sheikh started bidding on them.

No one was ever able to discover the precise fate that Bob, Dirk and Terry suffered at the hands of the MP's, but they weren't seen about the village for the next two days. Whether the American women kept them prisoner at their camp or they stayed there out of their own free will no one ever found out, but on the third day all three surfaced looking none the worse for wear. In fact they were wearing self-satisfied smiles and even Herpes seemed chirpier than usual.

Bert Hughes caught up with them in the pub at lunchtime.

"Well, well, been on a diet have we?"

"What do you mean?" asked Bob.

"Oh it's just that you three look as if you've lost weight!"

"That's not funny. A lot of help you were, I must say."

"Yeah Bert, we were abducted and you just stood by and let them get away with it!"

"Abducted? Who are you kidding? I'll bet you lot enjoyed every minute of it, being sorted out by a load of American women. I can't imagine what they must have done to you."

"No, I'm sure you can't. Anyway you've gone right down in our estimation so don't be asking us for any favours in future, you're on your own now."

"Favours? That reminds me, I've got a job for you three."

"Oh that's bloody typical, done nothing for us and now he wants us to do something for him."

"Well it's just that with all these people around someone's got to watch the river. The gamekeeper's got his hands full on the estate protecting the pheasants and the deer and I'm more concerned about some of the other problems the auction has created. I thought that you three might want to become unofficial water bailiffs for the next several days, that's all."

"Get lost, Bert," said Bob, "You've got nowt else to do now your traffic problem's solved, so do it your bloody self."

"Yeah, why would we be interested in helping someone who didn't help us in our hour of need?" said Dirk.

"Hour of need? Don't make me laugh. It wouldn't surprise me if I found you back at their camp tonight."

At that the three of them went quiet.

"Anyway I was really thinking of you lot. I mean let's say that out of these hundreds, if not thousands of people just one percent poach the river each night there won't be a salmon left for miles and we all know who'll suffer for a couple of months after that until the stocks build up again, don't we?"

It was a good point. Dirk and Terry's record night under the bridge had been just eight salmon and normally they only took one or two at a time. A couple of dozen people poaching over the next ten days could virtually wipe out the stock of fish in the area. They would be left with next to nothing to poach until a flood brought fresh fish in from the sea and who knew when that might be?

"We might go for an occasional walk along the river I suppose, but what would we do if we found any poachers?" asked Dirk.

"The boot would be on the other foot then, wouldn't it? You could either whistle me up or deal with it yourselves, within the law of course, or you could always set your lady friends on them!"

Bert chuckled, provoking spiteful looks.

"Seriously though, if you do it well I'll put you up for bailiff's jobs with the River Board after the auction. You could each do with some regular income and then you'd be out on the river all the time. That would be a lot safer than parading around here like red hot targets for heat seeking American MP's, now wouldn't it?"

They were not amused.

"Well I'm not a poacher or a fisherman," said Bob. "But if it gets you off our backs then I'll give it a go. The ferocious 'Erp will sort any poachers out, won't you 'Erp?"

He looked down at his dog, lying comatose and snoring under the table.

"Yes, I can see how he would. Well you can get on with it anytime you like because I saw some activity down past the Major's stretch this morning and just remember, doing a good job will get you my recommendation."

Bert Hughes had initiated the plan he'd been turning over in his mind for some time. Set a poacher to catch one. Who could be better at it than the wiliest of poachers in the district? They knew every trick in the book and every place to poach salmon for miles around. He knew the river was in good hands now and, if they did poach some fish for themselves, they wouldn't be taking many now they could plainly see his attention was well and truly focussed on them.

Hiroyuki Takada and his friend were hunting through the items for sale.

"So this is Shakespeare country?"

"Not exactly, but now that we are here we might as well find something to buy."

Takada was rummaging about in some cardboard boxes.

"Like what? This is junk. I do not think you have been completely honest with me, you know."

"You are right my friend, not completely honest. When I read about this auction I just fancied coming to see what I could find. I apologise to you that it's not very good, but we will enjoy some Shakespeare at the theatre in London, do not worry."

"So now I have to rummage around like a pig in a sty trying to find us something, but we don't know what, so that we can attempt to buy it?"

"Something like that, yes."

"I think you are going senile. However I shall persevere as I happen to like the best thing about this part of England."

"The people?" enquired Takada as his friend searched under a table.

"The people are OK, that I grant you. They are polite and helpful, quite the opposite to how they were in the war. No, it's not the people, it's that beer tanker."

"Ah yes, the beer tanker, only the British could organise an entire tanker of beer as a priority for such an occasion and the beer is not at all bad, is it my friend?"

There was no answer.

"Is it?"

Takada looked around. The other man slowly emerged from under the table holding a Japanese sword. Takada moved around the table and stopped his friend from drawing the blade, indicating that he should wait until the crowd thinned out a little. After a few minutes people drifted away from them and the blade was drawn.

"Wakizashi, Edo period. The blade is good, even if the handle is worn and what about these?"

They knelt and looked at the seven other swords lying under the table.

"My friend you have found us something very exciting, so much so that I will definitely be taking you to see some Shakespeare."

He was answered derisively. For the next half an hour they examined the swords. Some were a little rusted, but others were perfect and any damage they found could be repaired fairly easily.

"We need to have a serious think about our find. We need to go somewhere where we can meditate on the values of these. I mean they are obviously worth far more at home than they are here. Yes, we must find a place where we can think in peace and work out exactly how we are going to make sure of securing them."

His friend agreed and together they walked out of the marquee and headed straight for the beer tanker.

The Auction

The day the auction was to begin arrived under a clear blue sky.

By 8.00a.m. the beer tanker was under siege, Mickey's catering unit was serving bacon and egg rolls and mugs of tea as fast as they could go, a whole beef carcass was being turned over a large fire and the village green was burgeoning with people. Everywhere breakfasts sizzled on gas stoves, kettles boiled, rugs had been spread on the grass and numerous collapsible chairs and tables had appeared along with copious amounts of supplies for the day.

A man dressed as Abraham Lincoln was walking around on stilts, a magician was working card tricks from a small table while another man, dressed as Tarzan, was eating fire. Acrobats were tumbling and jugglers were juggling. Clowns wandered through the crowds playing jokes on people, making children laugh and creating a party atmosphere. It looked as though there was a travelling circus in the village because Charles and Nancy had found one over in the next county and Nancy had been there publicising the fact that its acts were liable to earn good money from the crowds at the auction and they were guaranteed to sell some tickets for their evening performances as well.

Mrs.Ferzakerley usually increased her income as a teacher at the Valley School by painting local scenes and selling them through the village store. However she and four of her lady friends had seen the coming auction as a money making opportunity not to be missed and they were selling cushions outside the village hall. The sign next to them read:

'Cushions for Bums – Beware of Hard Hall Seating!'

Their industrious production line had been stuffing and sewing for weeks. Bob was kicking himself that he hadn't thought of it. He had been so pre-occupied selling the tickets for the seats that he had completely missed this all too obvious earner. The ladies had set up shop and cornered the market and, at only four pounds a cushion, they were selling like hot cakes.

Farmers stood around the pens inspecting the various animals that were for sale and the village hall was surrounded by a human tide that ebbed and flowed around it. The stage and the storeroom were chock full of sale goods and there were more goods stacked outside ready to be passed in through the storeroom window as the pile inside diminished. The public address system whined with feedback as it was tested and the field telephones rang as their operators tried them out. The sea of people surged into the hall as soon as it opened at nine thirty.

Shipley was more than excited that the sale had grown into something so huge. He sat at his pulpit and examined the day's sale book, reading once more through the descriptions of some of the lots he was to sell. Montgomery had impressed him this time with his organisational skills and seemed to have handled everything perfectly. The seating arrangements, the public address system inside the hall and the marquee, the registration cards that had to be filled out by successful bidders, the production of the catalogue and the last minute entry sheets had all been taken care of by the very person he had been thinking of sacking. He would certainly keep young Charles Montgomery on if he could coordinate a sale like this.

As the seating filled up so did the space down either wall until the hall began to resemble a giant tin of tightly packed sardines. All was going well until two people found they had purchased tickets for the same seats. Faced with either fighting for their seats or having to stand all day they resolved to fight. As their fists flew Shipley banged his auctioneer's gavel on the pulpit and called for order. Charles tried to go and stop them, but couldn't get through the packed hall, then some more people found they too had been sold duplicate tickets to seats that were already occupied.

"Look here, I paid good money for these seats and I want them!"

"You what?"

Shipley was dismayed.

"Don't give me that you twerp or I'll come up there and knock your block off! I paid ten pounds each for these seats to your man and I'll be damned if I'm going to let someone else sit in them!"

"You paid what?"

Shipley looked at Charles whose astonishment was genuine.

"Did you charge people for these seats Montgomery?"

"No sir, no charge, I just gave the tickets to Bob and he sorted the whole thing out."

"Never mind you two having your own argument, I want my seats!"

With that tempers that had been simmering boiled over.

A woman with a hat pushed a man with a stick, the man with the stick hit another man with it who fell into some seated people whose seats jerked back into the knees of those sitting behind them who consequently pushed them back into those sitting in front. For a while the hall degenerated into a push and shove match as Shipley strove to maintain order. Those not involved did little to help matters by laughing at the participants, shouting encouragement and applauding them. Finally Shipley switched on the public address system, which yowled into life.

"Now stop that! D'you...ear me? Stop that...say! Hey you!"

He was now unwittingly speaking to the entire village as the PA system not only addressed everyone in the hall and the marquee, but also in the square, across the village green and in the pub as well.

The throngs of people automatically responded by asking,

"Who, me?"

"Yes, you, you...upid man!" boomed Shipley's voice.

"Stop behaving...*Crackle!*...school boy, will you? And you madam, kindly...hitting that gentleman with your handbag! Do come on! Ladies and Gentle...ease behave yourselves!"

"We are!" everyone shouted outside the hall as they began to realise what must be happening.

"Calm down everyone!" yelled Shipley into the microphone.

"We are calm!" they all yelled back.

Finally the people who were fighting in the hall either calmed down or ran out of steam. A man had a nosebleed, a woman had a torn dress and there were some bruises here and there, not least to people's egos. Disgruntled individuals who had lost their seats stood at the sides of the hall working out that those who had 'stolen' them would have to visit the toilets at some stage during the proceedings, so they would await their chance.

"Thank you...*Crackle!*...ank you everybody."

"No...ank you!" everyone shouted back.

So before the auction had started a kind of camaraderie was building amongst the thousands of people present. A bond had begun to grow between them helped by Shipley's not being aware that his voice was being transmitted all over God's creation and aided by the party atmosphere and the realisation that even with the best will in the world, this huge auction was likely to go wrong anyway. It was now ten minutes past ten, the start of the auction was already ten minutes late.

"Ladies and Gentlemen! Ladies and Gentlemen! Can I have... *Crackle!*...attention please!"

Many people stood to attention and some saluted.

"I'd like to...elcome you all here to...ttle Saddl...today and trust that you all had a pleasant...ney here. *Crackle!* We have a long day ahead of us so I'll...ust exp...the format of what you... do. When you...chase a lot you...a regis..tion form which you must...*Crackle!*...and hand back to the ...eers. If you wish to take what you have...chased with you, you will... for it at the offi... Bids from the...quee and outside the...will be...layed to me via the tele... So if that's all quite clear...further ado...*Crackle!*...begin."

People looked at each other seeking an explanation of what Shipley had said. The PA system seemed to be going on and off as he spoke. If they were going to have to put up with this all day then it was going to be a very long day indeed.

"Lot 1!"

A gigantic roar went up all around the village followed by a lot of laughter.

"Right, stop this auction!" yelled a man with a megaphone from the back of the hall.

"What the hell!" boomed Shipley through the PA system.

"I'm the Firemaster for this area! You are in contravention of the conditions of your Fire Certificate by having more than three hundred people in this hall! You will cease this auction immediately until I'm satisfied that all Fire Safety rules are being observed!"

"Oh my God!" boomed across the PA system.

"Right! All those who are standing will have to leave the hall immediately!"

Nobody moved.

None of them wanted to lose their places. They knew that once outside they would be resigned to the PA system alone without the chance of viewing the lots as they were held up or attracting the auctioneer's attention to any bid they might want to make.

Nobody moved.

"I said 'outside all of you who are standing'! This auction will not continue until you leave the building and I don't care whether that's today or next week, but this auction is stopped until you do!"

Very slowly people began to move out into the crowd in the square, pushing them back and adding to the crush. It took twenty minutes to get all of those who had been standing to leave the hall. Then the Firemaster, who in fairness was only doing his job, insisted on counting those seated, after which he said another eleven would have to leave.

But nobody wanted to be one of the eleven.

Eventually, after everyone in the hall had loudly complained that it should be everyone else who should leave, some of the people at the back begrudgingly complied so that the auction could start. However the Firemaster then insisted on checking the rear exit to the hall and found, much to Shipley's consternation, that it was locked.

"Until this door is opened Mr.Shipley you cannot continue. Were anything to go wrong in the hall people would be unable to get out quickly enough."

"Don't be ridiculous man, what on earth could possibly go wrong in the hall?"

"The point is that I need to be sure that people can get out swiftly before I can let you continue, so if you'll just get this door opened please."

No one could find the key.

Neither could anyone find any tools or a locksmith.

So it was decided they would have to break it down and three of the biggest, burliest men in the hall put their shoulders to it, but made absolutely no impression. It was a solid oak door with iron strapped hinges and a lock to match and it was not going to budge an inch. Eventually, with a slow hand clap breaking out all across the village, the old iron lock was picked by someone with a wire coat hanger and the door swung open to reveal a huge pile of garbage, broken furniture and smashed glass immediately outside.

"Right, this will all have to be cleared so that people can pass quickly around to either side of the hall and out of the way of everyone else should there be an emergency. It won't do as it is."

As Shipley continued to complain at the delay everyone mucked in to clear the rubbish. Finally the Firemaster was satisfied and they all returned to their seats. It was now coming up to midday and not one single item had been sold.

Crackle!

"I'm sorry ladies and...entlemen."

Groans from outside.

"But the...master has now been satis... o we...an get on with the...ale."

Loud laughter followed this statement and a cheer went up in the pub.

"And so...out further ado. Lot 1!"

Loud cheering erupted, but just as the first lot was held up and Shipley looked around the hall to take the first bid of the auction, his pulpit collapsed.

One second it was up there on the end of the stage with Shipley looking in full command, the next it went in three different directions at once with most of it flying into the people in the front row. Shipley went over backwards and disappeared, but not before exclaiming 'Jesus Christ!' loudly into the microphone.

"They're selling Jesus Christ as Lot 1!" people shouted to each other.

"That's not what it says in our catalogue!" other people shouted back.

Someone had loosened all the screws in Shipley's pulpit.

To this day no one has owned up, but loosened they were. Happily no one was injured by the collapse and Shipley only had his dignity dented. A screwdriver was found and people in the front row started rebuilding the pulpit and before long it was complete again.

Bzzzst! Crackle!

"...dies and...entlemen... I am...o...orry for all these...lays. Let us...again with...ot1!"

And so the great Rubicon & Shipley auction began, albeit late by some two and a half hours.

The first lot was a set of iron fire tongs valued at twenty pounds.

They sold for seventy.

No one could believe it.

There were just so many people who had all come to buy and were fully intending to purchase something that the prices were going to be greatly inflated. Bids came in over the telephones for the ensuing lots and gradually the auction speeded up. Soon there came an incorrect description in the catalogue which caused some consternation. Shipley had to sort it out with Charles and then confirm the correct description to everyone. Every so often there was another mis-described lot and Shipley began to reverse his original opinion about Charles' future back towards that of sacking him. The final straw came when a man in the front row stood up waving the colour insert sheet, claiming that one of the lots was misrepresented.

Charles paled.

"What on earth is that?" Shipley enquired into the microphone.

"What's what?" asked the man.

"Those pictures you're waving about. Where did you get them?"

"Don't be stupid, they're part of your catalogue and very good they are too, except that this is the wrong description for this particular lot."

"Montgomery, I want a word with you afterwards!"

"Yes Montgomery!" echoed around the hall and the village.

Charles went bright red.

"I want to know where those colour pictures came from!"

"Outer space!" shouted someone from the back of the hall.

"Who cares? Get on with it!" shouted someone else and Shipley, scowling at Charles, was forced to oblige.

Outside people were lunching, drinking and chatting merrily away to each other. Children were playing on the green in the sunshine. The PA system was worked on and became less crackly so everyone could finally understand what was going on. Bill Boyd took the Firemaster to the beer tanker and got him plastered, a state he would remain in for the rest of the week as every time he appeared to be even mildly sobering up someone would hand him another beer. Bert Hughes chatted up one of the MP's and Bob and Herpes kept well out of sight of Shipley, patrolling the river with Dirk and Terry.

The beef was cooked, carved and served. Both Mickey's pub and his service on the green went flat out all day and everyone settled into the way of the auction. Shipley kept it going until 6.30pm then wrapped it up having sold four hundred and eighty five lots, leaving him with only two thousand one hundred and thirty three to go as the arrival of people's last minute entries kept swelling the total.

Afterwards he looked everywhere for Charles, determined to find out about the colour photographs, but Charles had vanished, so he went into his back office and called Rawlston to inform him of the exceedingly high prices being paid for everything in the auction.

Eventually the village half emptied and returned to some kind of vague order. Not so the Flying Start which remained packed late into the night as its patrons swapped stories about the opening day of the Little Saddlington auction.

Day Two

On the Tuesday Shipley, having picked up a discarded colour insert, hunted for Charles before the auction got under way. He had confronted the secretary, waving the colour photographs in her face, demanding to know how they had come into being, but she had known nothing about them and said she was sure Mr.Montgomery could explain. However only after the auction had started and Shipley was stuck in his pulpit for the rest of the day did Charles appear.

Suddenly Shipley's voice vanished in the midst of conducting the bidding, although he kept on talking into what was now a dead microphone. He looked at Charles, who showed the greatest concern.

"G'day everyone!" boomed an Australian accent through the PA system.

"I'm just taking over for a few minutes from your Mr.Shipley, or Mr.Rip-Off as I call him, to tell you about me family heirloom that will be up for auction in the Flying Start pub tomorrow afternoon at three o'clock on the dot, so please make sure you haven't given all your money to Mr.Rip-Off by then. Some of you have seen it already, but for those of you who haven't I'll have a go at trying to describe it."

"Get this man off my system Montgomery!" Shipley yelled as Charles strenuously claimed to be out of control of what was going on.

"Well it's not that big, maybe six inches across and it has a winding handle set off to one side and a drum that goes around as you wind. It's got sort of pillars that hold the sides apart and a glass side plate so you can see all the cogs and springs inside, bit like a clock really. It's got a big, spiky thing sticking out of it and it's a golden colour on the outside with what I've been told is something called 'foliate engraving' all over it.

Now I can't tell you more than that and I have no idea what it is, just that it's been in my family for a very long time and I've brought it all the way from Australia to sell to one of you lucky people. So it's the Flying Start pub if you want to view it and tomorrow at three o'clock if you want to bid on it. You can see it at anytime in the pub between now and then.

Oh, and before I forget, we're organising a beer drinking contest on the green at the tanker. The heats are on Friday morning at eleven o'clock and the final is at one o'clock, so if you think you can drink three pints of beer quicker than I can then be there. It's a fiver each to compete and winner takes all. I think that's it, so now we can get back to the auction.

So it's back to you Mr.Rip-Off!"

As Bill Boyd ended his announcement Shipley's microphone came back on and caught him off guard.

"Get that bloody man off my... Oh dear! I'm so sorry about that ladies and gentlemen, I have no idea how that man got onto the system. Now then, perhaps we could continue without further interruption? Where were we?"

A mystery!

Bill Boyd had everyone fired up, it was as if half the village began moving towards the pub. As the first people entered they were shown to the bar, where the mystery object was on display, allowed to inspect it whilst any drinks they required were served and were then shown out of the side door back onto the village green. The size of the crowd trying to get to see the object did not diminish for the next three hours.

The Major had been busy packing the contents of his cottage with the help of Mrs.Ferzakerley. They had decided on everything that was to go with him to his new home and the remainder he had put into the auction to gain some funds. It had taken over a week to get everything properly organised and even then they'd had to repack what he was to take with him a number of times to reduce it to an acceptable amount.

Sadly he was having to part with many of the things that he and Margaret had loved and that reminded him of her, but he had been able to keep most of the photographs and they would look well on the walls of the room where he was intending to live. For a while his problem had been what to do about the great fish in its glass case until he decided that he would present it to the Flying Start on the Saturday before he made his final departure from Little Saddlington.

The auction would run for nine hours that day with Shipley taking just three fifteen minute breaks and he would manage to sell slightly under six hundred lots for such outrageous prices that the importance he had originally attached to the problem of the colour inserts began to fade.

"Lot number five hundred and sixty two ladies and gentlemen is one of 'Two Shagreen covered silver bound locked boxes, thought to possibly contain jewellery or precious metal'."

Shipley motioned Charles over to the pulpit.

"What on earth is this description Montgomery?"

As Charles looked up his entry forms the people in the hall became restless such was the pent up excitement about the two boxes and their unknown contents. Charles finally showed Shipley the entry form and received a filthy look in return.

"I'm sorry ladies and gentlemen we have a misprint in the catalogue descriptions for the next two lots which should both read 'thought to possibly have contained jewellery and precious metal'."

There was absolute uproar as those who had decided to have a go at buying the boxes had the wind taken out of their sails.

Willie Laird got to his feet.

"Excuse me!" he shouted at the auctioneer, trying to be heard over the commotion.

"Excuse me!"

"Yes? Can I help you?"

"Seeing as ye've made such a disaster with the description of this lot I doubt it, laddie, but anyway just try and answer me this question. Do ye, or do ye not know what is in the two boxes?"

Shipley spoke with Charles.

"Well, we're not quite sure what they contain."

"Not sure is it? Do I take it to be that ye might just have an idea then?"

"Well, we think they may contain some papers."

There was dismay in the hall.

"Think? Think do you? Somehow I doubt that very much! So, ye're 'not sure' and ye 'think' they may contain papers. But do ye know or don't ye?"

"Well, we're not sure, I mean we think, I mean we haven't been told precisely what the contents are."

"Aha! So it's just possible that perhaps the original description, the one ye now claim to be wrong, is in fact right! The boxes could indeed contain jewellery and precious metal, could they not?"

"Well, I suppose they could, but as I've said we just don't know."

"No, ye don't. But I think I'm right in saying that everyone here is going to do their very best to find out, aren't we lads?"

A resounding 'yes!' went around the hall as everyone realised the Scotsman had a point and that maybe there really were jewels or something else of value in the two boxes.

"Well get on with it, laddie, get on with it will ye?"

So Shipley began selling the first of the two mysterious boxes.

Willie Laird waited and let the bidding commence and then made his first bid at sixty pounds by making a small movement with his rolled up catalogue, intended only for the auctioneer to see. He was just about to bid again when he received a sharp prod from behind.

Swivelling round in his seat he found Julius Polperro sitting directly behind him with a cheeky smile on his face.

"Be careful Scotsman, you don't want to waste your money, now do you?"

Willie, now most concerned, turned back to the auctioneer.

Why had the Cornishman sat directly behind him? Was it to bid against him on the first box or to guage what to do on the second one? The bidding had reached one hundred and ten pounds. Willie wiggled his catalogue at the auctioneer again and, as he did so, Julius nodded to Shipley at the same time. Shipley took the bid, which was countered from the other side of the hall and so Willie wiggled again and Julius nodded and Shipley took the bid.

Willie was happier now he could see the auctioneer taking opposing bids from the other side of the hall and not from behind him. He continued to bid as the level passed two hundred pounds. He wiggled his catalogue at the auctioneer at two hundred and twenty pounds and Julius nodded again from his position behind Willie.

This time Shipley spotted Julius nodding and looked puzzled.

"Are you bidding, sir?" he asked as he looked at the two of them. Willie gave his catalogue a little wave in front of him, so that Julius could not see, and Julius nodded at Shipley.

"No, I mean you sir."

Again one waved and the other nodded.

Shipley pointed, seemingly at them both.

"No, you sir, are you bidding?"

Both Willie and Julius pointed at themselves as they tried to determine which of them was being addressed, but Shipley could not see Julius pointing at himself as he was for the most part hidden behind the Scotsman and so took it that he was not bidding.

"Very good, sir, I am taking your bid at two hundred and twenty pounds. Yes, you sir," he said to the Scotsman, but now both of them were convinced that the auctioneer was taking both of their bids. On went the bidding and each time the auctioneer looked to him for a bid Willie wiggled his catalogue in confirmation as behind him Julius nodded, blissfully unaware that Shipley was not including him in the proceedings. Shipley's eye was continuously looking for the small movement that Willie was making with his catalogue, but at three hundred and eighty pounds he again spotted Julius nodding.

"I must ask you again sir, are you bidding?"

The same performance was repeated, but this time Willie began to lose his temper, threw caution to the wind and stood up, yelling at Shipley.

"Ye blithering Sassenach! Of course I'm bidding! Have ye gone blind!"

"No sir! I have been taking your bids all along, it's the gentleman sitting directly behind you that I'm talking to."

"Oh it is, is it?"

Willie turned and looked at Julius sitting there pretending to be engrossed in his catalogue.

"So, it's games ye want to play is it?"

Julius looked up with a mock expression of surprise on his face.

"Me?"

"Aye, laddie, you! If it's a fight you want it's a fight you'll get!"

"Gentlemen please! Can I ask the gentleman sitting behind the Scottish gentleman if he is bidding on this item?"

Willie stood facing Julius, scowling at him, Julius didn't move.

"Aha! So, ye're beaten are ye? Good!"

He turned back to face the auctioneer and sat down with the result that Julius stood up nodding vigorously to Shipley and pointing at himself.

"Very good sir, thank you."

"Ye're welcome," said Willie unaware that Shipley was now taking Julius's bids as he started again. Then, as the price passed seven hundred pounds for the mysterious box with the unknown contents, Shipley was left with only the two of them bidding.

He took a bid from Willie with the wiggling catalogue and then another from Julius with the nodding head. Willie frowned as Shipley's gaze never seemed to have moved from him when he took the opposing bid, so he cautiously bid again. Shipley then picked up a counter bid from Julius so Willie, convinced the auctioneer had him bidding against himself and that he was being defrauded by Shipley, sprang to his feet.

"So ye devious English trickster! Ye've got me bidding against myself have ye?"

"No sir! Not at all! I'm taking bids from the gentleman directly behind you!"

"Directly behind me? Oh really, are ye now!"

He turned to Julius Polperro.

"So, ye sly little man, ye're trying to play games with me are ye?"

"Oh, I wouldn't bother playing games with you, you're far too busy playing with yourself!" replied Julius.

At that the Laird of the Highlands, desperate to buy the box he had convinced himself contained some great treasure, began throwing punches at Julius Polperro who obliged him by fighting back. Willie's two sons sitting on either side of him attempted to stop the fight, but Rory took a blow from Julius that had been aimed at Willie and made to hit back at the Cornishman. It was a pretty violent minute which ended when a uniformed policeman waded along the row of seats and broke it up by grabbing hold of both Julius and Willie and gave them both a good shaking.

"Control yourselves gentlemen, control yourselves! Otherwise I'll have to arrest you for causing a public disturbance. Settle down and let's sort this problem out. Now then, you, when you bid you wave your arms and you, when you bid you wave your catalogue about and then Mr.Shipley up there will be able to see which one of you is bidding. OK?"

The two of them, clearly extremely ruffled, confirmed their agreement to the policeman and so Sergeant Hughes asked Shipley to continue. Unable to get a bid out of either of them as the two men settled themselves down, he reminded them that the last bid had been from Julius. Willie desperately wanted the box but did not want to be forced to pay any more for it by the Cornishman.

"Look, why don't you buy this box and I'll buy the next one?" asked Julius, leaning forward.

"Ye'll no bid anymore?"

"Not if you give me your word you won't bid on the other one."

Despite the fact that Willie realised Julius was likely to buy the other box more cheaply without the two of them fighting over it, he wanted to be sure of at least buying one of them.

"Right you are then," he said.

So Shipley knocked the first box down to Willie Laird for seven hundred and eighty pounds and then, to Willie's great annoyance, Julius Polperro bought the second box for four hundred and sixty pounds. They made their way slowly through the packed hall to the front office to pay for their purchases.

"Now then Mr.Laird, Lot number five hundred and sixty two, that's seven hundred and eighty pounds plus 10% auctioneer's commission with 14% VAT on the commission. I'll just total that up for you."

"What! Ye cannot be serious lassie. Ye want me to pay more than I bid?"

The secretary was well used to dealing with people who queried Rubicon & Shipley's charges.

"We only charge you 10% sir, some auctioneers charge as much as 15% you know."

"Aye, and doubtless ye charge another 10% to the people who are selling things, I'm obviously in the wrong business."

"Well our advertising costs are very high."

"But the VAT rate is 8% surely?"

"Not any longer, the Chancellor of the Exchequer very kindly increased it in the Budget. Didn't you know?"

"Och I did hear some nonsense, but I never really pay much attention to that kind of thing."

Of course Willie Laird knew every financial detail of Geoffrey Howe's budget, he just didn't want to have to pay the English one penny more than he had to.

"We'll just have to pay our dues Scotsman, otherwise I'm sure this good lady won't be able to give us our receipts and we won't be able to claim our boxes."

"Aye, well I suppose we let ourselves in for it, I just hope we'll make our fortunes when we get them opened."

After obtaining their receipts they pushed their way back through the crowd to the side of the stage that the lots were being cleared from. Eventually their boxes were handed to them and they forced their way back down the hall and out of the main door.

"I'm sorry I hit ye, Cornishman, I just lost the head in there."

"We were both being stupid, if we'd got together beforehand we could have bought both boxes much cheaper and split the contents."

"Aye, that's a good point ye make. Now where shall we go to open them."

They looked around.

"Maybe to the pub? Then we could have a drink to celebrate?"

So they went to the Flying Start and attracted everyone's attention by placing the boxes on the bar. Mickey and Bill Boyd tried to open them, but neither of them could, even after using corkscrews, screwdrivers, nails and bits of wire.

"I've got a bunch of old keys on me somewhere, maybe one of them will fit," said Bob searching under his coat after they had been trying for a while.

"Here we are."

He tried various keys, but none of them fitted and then finally and miraculously one did and he unlocked the box. They were all amazed when the same key opened the second box. Willie and Julius stood before their prizes and together they lifted the lids and peered inside.

"What the hell is this?" asked Julius, pulling out a ladies' stocking filled with something and tied tightly every so often along its length, making it look like a string of sausages.

"And this?" said Willie pulling a gigantic daisy chain of paperclips from his box.

"Maybe there's something inside that," said Bob looking at the sausage stocking. Mickey carefully cut each of the sections open and emptied them on the bar. They were filled with sand and nothing else.

"Hard luck lads, how much did you pay for them?" asked Bob.

"Well together they work out at about fourteen hundred pounds."

Everyone in the pub began shaking their heads in disbelief and chiding them for their foolishness.

"You're not serious? Whatever possessed you?"

"Och, we just thought there might be gold or something valuable in them. In truth we were being very, very silly, anyway what's done is done. No hard feelings Cornishman?"

"None at all, Scottie, even if you do wear a skirt."

Willie eyed him suspiciously.

"Didn't mean it, want a drink?"

"Aye that I do, I think at this very moment I need a very large Highland Malt Whisky."

"Make that two of them would you please landlord?"

Standing there next to them Bob cleared his throat loudly.

"Oh and whatever our friend here is drinking. Thanks for getting the boxes open for us."

"No problem, guvnor, no problem at all," said Bob, ordering himself a large brandy.

Day Three

On the Wednesday Shipley started on time and his pace of selling took on some urgency as he realised that unless he got a move on he might not have everything sold even by the Saturday night. Twenty minutes after the auction commenced the National Anthem suddenly came blaring from the PA system. Shipley looked at Charles who, like everyone else, had no idea how or why or from where it was originating. Everyone got to their feet and stood respectfully until it had finished. Afterwards the auction continued with Shipley wondering if perhaps it was going to be repeated, but it wasn't and an hour later he moved to the window to sell that day's farm animals.

As usual the selling went well due to his being unable to miss a single bid from his vantage point. Pleased at his progress at having sold them, in what was for him record time, he moved back to the pulpit and continued at a rapid pace.

Above the hall a large, dark cloud had been growing almost imperceptibly all morning. The auction had been blessed with glorious sunshine from the start, but shortly before lunchtime the heavens opened as a summer thunderstorm deluged the village.

There were very few places for people to take refuge.

Those with caravans ran to them, those with tents attempted to keep dry in them. Hardly anyone had vehicles to shelter in with them all being parked outside the village and so the hall, the marquee and the pub swiftly became packed to over capacity. The vast amount of people simply had to suffer the rain. Everyone in the hall, being bone dry, thought this was great fun as they could hear the shrieks and cries from those outside who were getting a good soaking.

"I'm sorry about this ladies and gentlemen, I hope you can all manage to..."

There was a loud crackling sound and a flash amongst the electrics outside the hall and the PA system shorted out. Shipley explained that he couldn't continue the auction with only the participation of those in the hall so they would have to be patient and wait for the storm to pass. Water from the roof began dripping inside the hall as outside the torrential English summer rain hammered down. It was amusing at first, picturing the chaos of those who were getting wet outside, but then the drips of water inside the hall began to increase in number and volume. It was impossible for anyone, seated or standing, to move out of the way of them as the hall was packed extra tight by those who had crushed inside to escape the rain. They could only remain where they were in trepidation as more and more water began dripping on them, the loud peals of thunder that shook the hall and flashes of lighting only adding to their concern.

"Hey, we're all getting wet! We'll be electrocuted if this place gets struck by lightning!" one extremely helpful person shouted.

"Let's get out of here!"

However those at the doorway were reasonably dry and were not going to go back out into the pouring rain, even though those who were seated suddenly had rivulets of water showering down on them. Inevitably another push and shove match started. This time Shipley had no sound system to assist him in trying to bring things under control and the jostling quickly erupted into full scale fighting as water suddenly came cascading down from the ceiling. Blows were exchanged with those near the doorway and the crowd made a determined surge at them in an effort to break out of the hall.

However the front door brigade were not going to be easily pushed from their dry refuge and defended their position with the utmost vigour. They linked arms and some thirty of them wedged themselves in the doorway and the space next to the front office. Presented with a solid, fairly impenetrable wall of resistance those who had paid for their seats had no option but to endure their rainwater shower.

Mercifully whilst this spectacle of people striking out at one another to avoid getting wet was underway the thunderstorm passed over Little Saddlington and the sun came out again. The people in the doorway unlinked their arms and moved out into the square and the hall was able to slowly disgorge its now thoroughly dampened contents. Water was pouring from more than a dozen places in the roof.

"Whatever is going on Montgomery? We've never had leaks in the roof before. I spent a lot of money doing it up only recently."

"Maybe it was struck by lightning and some of the slates were dislodged Mr.Shipley?"

"This is hopeless, look at all the water in here, you better get some mops and start clearing it up. I'll go and see if I can get the public address system working."

"Oh let me go and do that Mr.Shipley! The secretary can start organising the clean up. You just leave it all to me."

Charles ran out of the hall, desperate that Shipley should be stopped from nosing around the PA system, where he might find that it was hooked up to far more places than it was supposed to be. He also hoped that he wouldn't be sent up onto the roof and have to replace all the slates he had so painstakingly removed before the auction.

The storm created yet another long delay and even when the people re-entered the hall water was still dripping from the roof. All kinds of bowls, buckets and kitchen pans that had been quickly dug out by local people were located throughout the hall and the sound of dripping water plinking into them accompanied the auction for a considerable time as it once more got under way.

"'Ere Charles."

"Bob, I've been looking everywhere for you! What do you mean by selling the seating tickets for a tenner each? Shipley's furious."

"Oh, is he? Good. It's inflation Charles, that's all."

"Inflation? Greed more like and you'd got the brass neck to give us our cut out of a fiver a ticket."

"Yes, well I'll make the money up to you both, you know I will."

"Oh yes?"

"Look never mind all that now, we can sort it out later, I've come for my pay out."

"What? You want it right now?"

"Well I thought I'd strike while the iron's hot."

"You'll end up a millionaire one of these days if you're not careful."

"I'm always careful son, come on, I could do with the cash."

Charles looked at the secretary and shook his head.

"He 'could do with the cash' when he must be rolling in it."

"Come on you two, never mind getting clever! What about my money?"

"Alright, keep your shirt on, let's look it up. Now then, lot numbers five sixty two and five sixty three Mr.Fotherdew. You've used a few beauties at these auctions Bob, but where on earth did you get the name Fotherdew from?"

"Just came to me, at least it puts Shipley off the scent. Thanks for the 'mis-cataloguing' by the way."

"There's a lot more than mis-cataloguing going on at this auction, Bob."

Bob frowned.

"You're not getting yourself into trouble are you lad?"

Charles was making out one of Shipley's pre-signed cheques they made quick payouts with.

"Between you and me I'm quitting straight after the auction.

"Good for you, it's about time you went and married that bit of stuff of yours before someone else snaffles her."

"Bob!"

"Well she's a tidy piece so she is. I reckon you'd be mad to lose her. Give her some kids, you know, make her happy!"

The secretary blushed.

"Listen, that's enough out of you. Expert on marital affairs are we all of a sudden?"

"Not really, my time's over for all that I guess."

"That's not what I heard, can you whistle 'Dixie' yet, or is it 'Old Man River'?"

"Oi! That'll be enough from you, come on, let's have the cheque."

"Here you are Mr.Fotherdew, sir. You're sure Mickey will cash it?"

"Yeah, no problem, by the way you should've seen their faces when I opened the boxes for them."

"Weren't they suspicious?"

"Nah, they were so happy to get them opened and then so shattered when they saw what was in them that it never occurred to either of them they might've been mine all along. It was a pretty good deal, considering I bought them for twenty quid each."

"I'll say it was, what did you put inside them?"

"Junk mate, absolute junk. I'll let you have your cut this evening."

"OK Bob, be lucky."

"And you, you young devil and hurry up and marry that Nancy of yours, will you?"

There seemed to be no more disturbances at the auction and so Shipley worked up a good rhythm of selling, moving along at a fairly fast rate once more. But in mid-afternoon the National Anthem once again blared out from the speakers, stopping him in the middle of taking bids on one of the better paintings in the auction. As they all sat down he found that once more his microphone was not working.

"Well here I am again folks, good as my word!" boomed an Australian voice from the speaker system.

"It's three o'clock and all's well and I'm going to auction me heirloom right now. You can bid from the marquee or the beer tanker as we've set up our own phone lines."

Shipley gave up.

He sat there abjectly trying to ignore what was happening, but the booming voice wouldn't let him.

"Oh, and Mr.Rip-Off you can carry on just as soon as I'm finished, alright?"

Shipley gazed forlornly out of the window.

"Now then I've got some bods here in the pub who seem to be seriously interested so I'll see if I can get a bid out of one of them to start off with. No Bob, I am not going to swap it for your dog. Now please be serious ladies and gents. Who wants to start the bidding?"

The Scotsman looked at the Cornishman.

The Cornishman looked at the Grubb brothers.

The Grubb brothers looked at the object.

"Come on, come on! Someone must want to open the bidding. One of you must want it. Crikey! This is like pulling hen's teeth!"

One of the phones rang.

"A bloke in the marquee bids a tenner!" proclaimed Mrs.Mickey proudly.

"Twenty!" said the Scotsman.

"Thirty!" said the Cornishman.

"Forty!" said Maurice Grubb.

"This is more like it folks. We've got a bid of forty pounds right here in the pub. No, now it's fifty to the Scotsman... Sixty, seventy..."

"One hundred!" said Mickey, who was taking bids from the beer tanker.

"And fifty!" said the Scotsman.

"One seventy five!" said Mrs.Mickey.

"Two hundred!" said Maurice Grubb and they were truly off and running as bids began to come in fast and furious. Head to head the Scotsman, the Cornishman and the Grubb brothers ran the bidding up against those in the marquee and at the beer tanker. Flying along trying to keep track of it all Bill and his missus were having great fun enjoying the chase. They were laughing, cajoling and encouraging those in the pub to bid more, taking the bids as they were called from the phones and trying to control the crazy thing they had unleashed.

Before long the bidding had passed two thousand pounds.

"Wait a minute everyone! Hold it! Hold it! Stop the bidding! The price has passed my missus' reserve price of two thousand pounds so someone is definitely going to buy me heirloom!"

A great cheer went around the gathering.

"But I'm so excited I need a drink so we're going to stop and have a quick one and I suggest you all do the same."

In the village hall Shipley held his head in his hands as yet another great cheer could be heard from outside. Drinks were served and those who wanted to buy Bill's heirloom used the opportunity to work out their finances and game plan. Everyone was talking of nothing but 'the object'.

Bill's voice finally came back over the speakers.

"OK, well we feel a lot better for that and we hope you do too. Now then, the bidding had reached two thousand one hundred pounds from someone in the marquee called 'Mr.Trump' so can anyone now please trump Mr.Trump?"

"Two two!" said the Scotsman.

"Two three!" said the Cornishman.

"Two four!" said Maurice Grubb and they were off again, even if the bids were coming in a little slower now with them going up in increments of a hundred pounds. After a few minutes the bidding slowed right down and gradually the phones went quiet as those outside gave up and the contenders in the pub were left to fight it out. The figure of three thousand five hundred pounds was passed, which was a great deal of money especially considering no one knew what the object actually was. The bids trickled back down from hundreds to fifties to twenties between the Scotsman, the Cornishman and the Grubb brothers. Then it was tenners and then fivers as they stood in a huddle outbidding each other.

"Well I'm sorry to see it go, whatever it is, but I'm out!"

"The Cornishman drops out at three thousand seven hundred and eighty pounds everybody!" boomed the speakers.

A roar went up across the green. Those packed into the pub looked expectantly at the Scotsman and the Grubb brothers.

"Ye don't really want this thing now do ye, lads?" said the Laird of the Highlands, "Why don't you both just drop out and let me take it back to Scotland?"

Horace looked at Maurice.

"Four thousand pounds!" they said in unison.

The Scotsman shook his head in disappointment and indicated to Bill they had won.

"It looks like these two gentlemen are going to be the proud owners of me heirloom, whatever it is, for four thousand pounds. Going once! Going twice! Going..."

"Five thousand pounds!"

There was total disbelief as a slight, dapper looking man wearing a suit and tie stepped forwards.

"Would you like to bid higher gentlemen?" he said to the Grubbs, who looked at each other.

"Well, no, I don't think we would against that high a bid," said Horace.

"We think we'll pass on it, I mean we don't even know what it is, we just got a bit carried away really," said Maurice.

"So am I free to purchase this 'item' at a price of five thousand pounds with, I believe, no extras to pay on top?"

"Well blow me folks! There's a bloke here's going to pay five thousand pounds for me family heirloom! I can hardly believe it!"

"Neither can I!" said Shipley as he sat dejectedly at his pulpit.

A great cheer went around the green and the marquee and applause came rippling back into the pub. Everyone congratulated everyone, Bob offered Herpes to Bill for his heirloom one last time and the dapper man got out his cheque book.

"Cheque alright?"

"Well I don't exactly know you, do I mate?"

"Oh this one won't bounce, you see I'm from the British Museum of Piscatoriana."

"Piscatory....what?"

"Piscatoriana, old fishing things if you like."

"And that's what this is, an old fishing thing?"

"Reel actually, it's an old fishing reel made in London in the 1800's specifically for the King."

"The King? Strewth!"

"Yes, it was made by a famous clockmaker, hence the blued mechanism with that wonderful crystal side exposing it, all worked from the offset crank handle. That big spike went through a hole in the handle of the rod and was secured in place with a wing nut. It was finished in gilt as you can see and was known simply as 'the King's Golden Reel'. It's written up in various reference works. There was a silver one as well, which is now held in a private collection. This one was exhibited at the Great Exhibition of 1850 in London and featured prominently in the exhibition, but has been missing ever since. We are very, very pleased to get our hands on it I can tell you."

"And we've had it all these years not knowing. So it's going to be put on show where everyone can see it? Good on you, mate. This is really great, the King of England, doll, can you believe it?"

He put his arm around his wife and everyone watched as the man completed the British Museum of Piscatoriana official cheque and handed it over along with his business card, wrapped the object in a linen cloth, placed it in his briefcase, bade them good day and left the pub.

"Well folks!" boomed the Australian voice, "It looks like the drinks here in the pub are on me for the rest of the day! I'll even buy one for Mr.Rip-Off! You can have your speakers back now and feel free to carry on whenever you like."

Shipley found that his microphone came back on and he attempted to get on with the sale, but it was all such an anti-climax that re-generating interest in the auction was extremely difficult. Horace and Maurice were both shaking hands with Bill and congratulating him.

"What are you going to spend it on, Bill?" asked Horace.

"Dunno. I'd like to have bought an old car and shipped it back with us, but the vehicles in the auction are pretty hopeless. I guess me and the missus'll go to London and try to buy one on our way home."

"Ooh, you don't want to buy a car in London," said Maurice.

"No, very expensive it is, you'll pay through the nose for old cars down there. Why don't you come up to Lancashire and have a look at some of ours?"

"Yours?"

"Yes, we've got a lot of old stuff and we wouldn't mind selling one or two things to a bloke like you, for a reasonable price like."

"I don't know gents, we've decided to go to London to try and find the missus some antiques seeing as those in the auction aren't up to much."

"Oh we've got loads of antiques, she'd have a real good time looking at everything at our place."

Bill wasn't too sure. Lancashire was way up in the North of England wasn't it? He wouldn't want to drag his wife up there on a wild goose chase.

"It seems a long way to go, have you got much that's really special?"

Horace looked at Maurice.

"We've got an old Lagonda."

"A... Lagonda?"

"Yes."

"You wouldn't...by any chance...be talking about an Aston Martin Lagonda, would you?"

"Yes, it's an old 1936 Drophead Coupe. Then there's an MGTA and an old Bentley and a number of others."

"1936? A 1936 Drophead Coupe?"

Bill held onto the bar to steady himself.

"An MGTA? A Bentley? I think I need a drink."

His wife came up to him and he put his arms around her.

"These gentlemen have a Coupe, I mean an Aston, a 1936 Drophead. An Aston Martin doll, a 1936 Drophead Coupe!"

She smiled, knowing how hopeless he was when it came to old cars.

"Now you promise me you've got some antiques for the missus?" he asked the two Lancashire Lads.

"Oh loads of them, she can take her pick. We're leaving on Sunday morning and we could take the two of you with us if you like."

"Done! Looks like we're going to Lancashire doll, wherever that is," said Bill, hugging his wife.

Day Four

"At least they're not using a net."

"No, they're sniggering fish."

"It's 'snagging' fish, isn't it?"

"I thought it was 'sniggling'."

"Whatever you want to call it attaching big lumps of lead to treble hooks and dragging them across the river is illegal."

As Bob, Dirk and Terry watched them one of the poachers foul hooked a salmon, the extreme bend in the rod showing that heavy line was being used. The fish leapt violently across the middle of the pool in desperation to keep facing upstream. As it was dragged unmercifully backwards towards the shingle its struggling tore the hook free and it raced back into the depths, followed by an expanding 'V' trail on the surface.

"That one got away at any rate. Can you see any fish on the bank they've already got?" asked Bob.

"No, none, they'll have them hidden if they've got any," replied Terry.

"There's five of them that I can see against the three of us and the 'Erp," said Dirk.

"We're too far from the village to go back and get Bert, they'd be gone by the time we returned."

"Well what are we going to do? I don't fancy getting my head split open just because Bert wants us to save a few salmon."

"No, but if we did get ourselves bailiff's jobs we'd be facing situations like this all the time, so we've got to think of something," said Bob.

"But if we were bailiffs we'd get guns, wouldn't we?" asked Dirk.

"Don't be stupid, who's going to trust us with guns?"

"Well they'd have to give us something, how would we be supposed to deal with gangs of poachers with just the 'Erp?"

"Maybe the 'Erp could arrest them," said Bob facetiously.

"What do you think 'Erp? Come on me old mucker, show us what to do will you?" said Terry, roughing Herpes up around his face and head. The 'Erp replied by placing one of his front legs over Terry's arm and playfully trying to bite his hand and as he did so he let out a growl.

"'Ere, we could pretend the 'Erp's really dangerous, maybe that would scare them off."

Bob looked at his dog.

"Yeah Bob, we'll go out there, you pretend to be holding the 'Erp off, as if he really is dangerous, and we'll give them some mouth and maybe they'll go."

"It's not that it's a bad idea lads, it's just that I don't really know about the 'Erp, I mean when all's said and done he is a bit unpredictable. Anyway what do we do if they don't go?"

"I reckon they'll go Bob, everyone's scared of dogs, anyway they'll be keen to leave once they've been discovered."

At that Herpes, who was still playing with Terry, barked at him, signalling their presence to the poachers.

"Bloody hell! We'll have to do it now! You stupid animal! Come on then, let's

94

get 'em!"

The three of them strode out of the bushes with the 'Erp trailing in their wake and walked towards the river bank with all five poachers staring at them.

"Right lads!" shouted Bob, "What you're up to is illegal!"

"Yeah, illegal!"

"You can either pack it in and move on or you'll have to come with us to the police station!"

"Who the hell are you?" shouted one of the poachers as he stood up to his waist in the river.

Bob paused.

"River bailiffs!"

The poachers started laughing.

"River bailiffs? You look more like gypsies! Where's your identity cards then?"

"Bloody hell, he's right," whispered Dirk.

"We can't prove we're bailiffs. Now what do we do?"

"The dog Bob, the bloody dog!" hissed Terry.

Bob turned to Herpes.

"Will you get back? Get back I say! Back!"

Herpes tilted his head to one side, looked quizzically at his master and wagged his tail, thinking to himself 'What do you mean 'get back'? Back where? We're going this way, aren't we?'

"Ferocious dog here lads, you'd better move on or he'll tear you to bits!" Terry yelled at them.

"Bollocks! Looks more like a flea bitten fur rug to me! That thing couldn't fight its way out of bed."

Bob berated his dog.

"Will you get back? Back you wild animal, back I say! I might not be able to hold him much longer lads!"

'What the hell are you shouting about?' thought Herpes, 'You never normally shout at me. Everyone else does, but you don't. I mean we're mates you and me, aren't we?'

All five poachers began to wade slowly out of the river towards them.

"Christ, they're bloody coming!"

"Gerroutovit!" screamed Bob at Herpes, "Get back! He goes mad when he's riled!"

"It'll be the worse for you lot if the dog goes for you!" shouted Dirk as the five men clambered out of the river and faced them.

"Do as I say! Get back, will you! Back!"

'Oh I see, it's a game is it? Not like you to want to play games, but if you really want to play then here goes.'

Herpes ran at Bob and jumped up at him.

"Blimey!" said Bob never having had the 'Erp do that before and pushed him away.

"Get back you mad dog! Back! Do you hear me!"

'Of course I can hear you. Funny kind of game this.'

"I can't control him!" shouted Bob.

"He can't control him!" shouted the other two as the poachers began to walk towards them.

"This isn't supposed to be happening, do something Bob!"

'A game, a very silly game. You stand there and shout at me for doing nothing. Oh well, shout away and I'll just keep jumping on you.'

As the 'Erp leapt at Bob again his master, desperate to impress the poachers that the 'Erp really was dangerous, aimed a kick at him and unfortunately his boot connected.

'Ow! That bloody hurt! I thought we were playing a game! So you're going to change the rules without warning and start kicking me are you? Not today you're not!'

As the pain from the kick checked the 'Erp back and the ignominy of being kicked by his master made him smart, his demeanour began to change.

"That'll teach you! Let that be a lesson! Shouldn't have tried to bite me, should you?"

"See! He even bites his own master! Mad he is! He'll tear you to pieces if you come any closer!" shouted Dirk.

The poachers, seeing bob kick out at Herpes, were impressed and stopped in their tracks. Terry had been right, none of them wanted to tangle with a vicious dog. Bob stood between Dirk and Terry facing back at Herpes and kicked out at his dog again.

"Didn't like that, did you? But a bit of boot is all you understand, isn't it? Get back I say!"

He kicked out at the 'Erp once more, but he was making a really serious mistake.

The 'Erp, who loved his master and was devastated at being shouted at and kicked, felt Bob's boot brush his ribs and that was it. He began to lose control.

'So you're going to turn on me, are you?'

He started to growl.

'Kick an old friend when you've lured him into playing a game, would you?'

His top lip curled back.

'If you think this is how it's going to be from now on you've got another think coming, pal!'

His hackles began to rise and he fixed Bob with an evil eye.

"Jesus!" exclaimed Bob as he witnessed the sudden change come over the 'Erp.

"What the..."

Herpes was growling at him.

Each time he drew breath his rib cage forcefully expanded and contracted as the growls grew louder and more threatening. The 'Erp was now deadly serious. His fangs were exposed, his hackles were raised and his body language indicated a dog that was gathering itself to attack.

"Calm down! Pull yourself together!" shouted Bob to no effect.

"The dog's gone bloody mad!"

"The dog's gone bloody mad!" echoed Dirk and Terry.

"No he really has!" yelled Bob.

"Yes he really has!" they echoed again.

"Get back 'Erp! I don't think I can hold him!"

"He doesn't think he can hold him!"

"We can see that!" shouted one of the poachers as they began backing away.

"I haven't seen him like this before!"

"He hasn't seen him like this before!" echoed Dirk and Terry as behind them Herpes had now completed his transformation into his own version of the terrifying Hound of the Baskervilles.

"He's getting ready to attack! Someone do something!"

"He's getting ready to attack! Someone do something!" they echoed as Bob backed into them.

"No! He really has gone mad!" yelled Bob.

"No! He really has gone mad!" they echoed.

"For Christ's sake look out!"

"For Christ's sake look out!" they shouted as Herpes' growling erupted into a broadside of angry barking, his final warning that it was all over for all of them as he teetered on the brink of launching a pre-emptive nuclear strike.

'Think you can take me for granted, do you? I'll teach you to play a nasty trick on an old mate! Kick me would you? Let's see how you like some of this!'

"He's lost it! Run! Run!" screamed Bob as he burst between Dirk and Terry.

"He's lost it! Run! Run!" they shouted as Bob cannoned into the poachers. The two of them had taken the 'Erp's growling and barking simply to be his going along with their scheme to frighten the poachers, but they took one look at the terrifying denizen that came charging at them, slaver pouring from its jowls, it's attack guided by crazed radar eyes, its rigid coat sticking out like a porcupine's quills, its fangs bared ready to gorge on them for lunch and they took off, knocking over a couple of poachers as they went.

Herpes launched an all out attack on the eight of them, biting anything that moved, snarling, barking and completely out of control.

"It's only us 'Erp!" yelled Dirk and received a sharp bite to his ankle.

"Aaaah! He really has lost it!"

"I kept telling you, but you just kept repeating what I was saying like a pair of bloody parrots!" shouted Bob as they sprinted along the river bank.

Herpes was attacking one of the poachers as the men scrambled to get away from him. They ran helter skelter down a slope, shouting at the dog to stop, but it was they who had to stop upon suddenly finding themselves facing a riverside cliff that rose sixty feet straight up from the water's edge.

"Oh no! Deadman's Drop!" shouted Terry.

"Deadman's Drop! What do you mean?" shouted one of the poachers.

"Well that's what we call it! There's no way around!"

Behind them a loud growling, a horrendously evil sound could be heard. Herpes had them cornered as he came stalking down the slope, daring any of them to try and get past him.

'I've got you now! You lot have had it! Let's see what you make of this!'

The 'Erp rushed at them, roaring, snarling, barking and scattering shingle and sand as the men backed into the river.

"For pity's sake call your dog off mate! We'll come quietly!"

"I can't call him off! I kept telling you! He's gone bloody mad!"

"We must be able to get round that cliff!" shouted another one of the poachers.

"You can try it if you want, but if you slip it'll be a pine box you'll be needing!"

"Why!"

Dirk and Terry looked at each other and back at the poacher.

"The Weir Pool!"

Herpes kept rushing at them, a rabid, ferocious, frenzied animal putting on a menacing display until they were all backed well out into the river.

"We can get across the river here, can't we?"

"No mate, it's too deep and the current's far too strong out in the middle, you'll get swept away."

"Yeah and don't bother trying to swim for it either because round that corner is the Weir Pool. They say that once you go in there, there's only one way you come out!"

"Well we can't stand in here all day just because of a bloody dog!"

The poacher began to wade out towards Herpes. The 'Erp went berserk, the furore he put up accompanied by white, snapping fangs ready to rip and tear along with evil eyes that bored into their target was enough to frighten the toughest of men.

The man waded back.

Herpes quietened.

"'Erp it's only us, there's a good dog," coaxed Terry.

Herpes fixed him with an evil stare and growled, raising his hackles again.

"You've got to do something Bob, we can't stand in the river for long, it's alright for these blokes they're wearing chest waders." said Dirk.

"What do you suggest? He's gone completely out of control. Just look at him."

They looked at the dog, knowing all too well that Bob was right.

'So now I've got you in the river how does it feel? Going to kick me again are you? I don't think so and not for a very long time to come, but just to make sure I get some respect in future I'm going to keep you there until you say you're sorry. Until you say you're really, truly, sorry.'

"How long do you think he'll keep us here Bob? This water's bloody freezing," said Terry, beginning to shiver.

'Now I do like this game,' thought Herpes.

The Sheikh had found Mrs.Ferzakerley, who was taking charge of a large group of children while their parents attended the auction, and had left his son with her while he went into the hall with his men. They pushed their way through the crowd right to the front row, which was fully occupied. Undeterred they stood looking expectantly along the row at the people sitting there as if everyone should move out of the way. But they simply looked back at the Arabs, none of them intending to move after paying Bob's levy. The Sheikh cleared his throat, but still no one moved. He made a small movement with his hand, the daggers were drawn, brandished and people got swiftly out of the way.

"Thank you good people!" he said, interrupting Shipley as the three of them walked to the centre of the row and sat themselves down. Shipley, noting the Sheikh's appearance, drank some more of his honey and lemon drink, the only way he could keep from losing his voice after his days of auctioneering, and went straight to the swords.

"The next lot is an extra lot, number one thousand eight hundred and sixteen 'A'. A collection of old swords, thought to be Japanese."

Towards the back of the room Takada and his friend glanced at each other but their expressions did not change. Charles hunted through the catalogue and the late entry sheets, but couldn't find where this particular lot had suddenly sprung from.

"Now what am I bid for these ladies and gentlemen, shall we say one hundred pounds to start me? One hundred pounds?"

Takada put in a bid and there was a lull, surely they were not going to sell for a hundred pounds?

"One hundred and twenty," said Shipley eagerly taking a bid from the Sheikh. Takada bid again and so did the Sheikh. They continued to bid as the price rose towards one thousand pounds, passed through it and continued on upwards, now in increments of fifty pounds a bid. Shortly it passed through two thousand pounds.

"Who can possibly be bidding against us?" asked Takada.

"I think it's the Arab."

"I wonder if he knows what they're worth?"

There were only the two of them making bids, but the Sheikh kept right on firing in counter bid after counter bid. Four thousand pounds was passed, then five, six and seven. Everyone's attention was held by this unexpected upwards spiral. Ten thousand pounds was passed, then fifteen and then twenty thousand.

Takada began to sweat.

"I think we are going to lose this my friend, he just continues and continues."

"But think of the disgrace if we fail to buy them!"

"It will only be a disgrace if anyone in Japan gets to hear about it."

When the Sheikh made a bid at a stupendous twenty seven thousand pounds Takada decided he was not going to be able to better the Arab and threw in the towel, leaving Shipley delighted not to have to invent bids against the Sheikh now that the swords had attained three times the price Rawlston had placed on them. The two Japanese were despondent. They had planned meticulously, calculating the values of each sword right down to the last Yen.

With no intention of making a profit had they been successful, seeking only the honour of repatriating the swords to present to their favourite museum, they had not taken into account the unlikely possibility of having an Arab Sheikh bidding against them.

They had travelled all that distance and made such a spectacular find only to lose it. They walked dejectedly out of the hall and headed across the square to the beer tanker. As they quaffed their beers Takada said,

"I feel I need something stronger than this."

At that moment one of the female MP's came up to the General and Hetty Joy who were standing outside the hall and saluted.

"General, sir!"

"Yes corporal, what can I do for you?"

"The General and Mrs. Verbeer's presence is requested on the village green, sir!"

"It is? Do you have any idea why, corporal?"

"No, sir! Just that it's urgent, sir!"

"Alright then, lead on corporal."

The General was interested to find out the reason behind this urgent request and he and his wife followed the corporal through the square. Once out on the green the corporal stopped, turned, saluted again and said,

"If the General will just remain here, sir!"

"Here?"

Chuck and Hetty Joy looked around. There were just the usual droves of people milling about in the sunshine listening to the auction.

"Yes, sir!"

"Very well corporal, we'll wait here then."

He looked at his wife, neither of them could see anyone who seemed to be looking for them, but they remained there as requested.

It was barely two minutes later when the percussion started.

A deep, resonating bass drum and numerous snare drums pounded into life and, before the General or anyone else had time to realise what was going on, a sixty piece American marching band catapulted into life and people ran in every direction as they came advancing in short, quick steps out onto the green from behind the beer tanker. With drums pounding, brass blaring and instruments swinging from side to side they arrived opposite the General and his wife, turned and then marched off towards the river, scattering people before them. A minute later they were breaking up and marching in intricate patterns, never lessening their pace or the quality of their playing as the huge crowd looked on. Back towards the General and Hetty Joy they came forming a crescent shape, peeling off from either end and reforming into a complex phalanx before heading back towards the river. They turned and marched to the right, turned and marched to the right, turned and marched to the right and turned and marched to the right again. It was all so fast and completed with such polished ease and precision. For almost fifteen minutes they held the crowd spellbound and then they suddenly stopped.

To a single snare drum beat they marched silently up to the General and his wife.

"General Verbeer, sir! The Combined American Forces European Marching Band would be proud to take your salute, sir!"

Chuck Verbeer was standing to attention.

His arm came up and the band returned his salute. It was a strange, emotional moment there on the village green with the crowds looking on. After some seconds the General's arm dropped to his side, the snare drum beat again and the band marched forward, passing to either side of the two of them.

"If you'll follow us, sir!"

Through the square and up the steps of the hall they marched straight into the auction with several hundred people intent on following them. Shipley was going full bore selling a three piece suite when the band forced their way in. One second there was not enough room for those standing at each side of the hall, the next there seemed to be plenty as people shrank back against the walls to make way for the musicians. Shipley faltered at the interruption, got the bidding going again and then blew his top as he lost his way.

"What on earth do you people think you're doing?"

But instead of answering him the band went into a fast version of 'When You're Smiling' and drowned him out. Immediately, out of nowhere, twelve cheerleaders dressed in bright green and gold outfits and holding multicoloured Pom Poms aloft sprang onto the stage and went into a dance routine. The General and Hetty Joy, delighted by this spectacle, stood at the back looking on admiringly.

Shipley sat there gawking, his eyes and mouth wide open as nubile female bodies paraded themselves on the stage right next to him. They opened even wider a few minutes later when, in one swift movement the cheerleaders removed their outfits, each revealing a skimpy, glittering bikini beneath. Now everyone in the hall had their eyes and mouths wide open as the women cavorted and twirled around on the stage and the band stepped up the pace. Five minutes of vibrating music and voluptuous movement later the cheerleaders danced off the stage and followed the band out of the hall and down the steps to where the General and Hetty Joy were now standing. They formed up and stood to attention as the 'Star Spangled Banner' was played followed by the British national anthem. The band saluted and marched off and the cheerleaders waved to the General and exited through the crowd. Chuck and Hetty Joy were left to reflect on the unexpected, rousing exhibition they had just witnessed as Shipley's voice came back over the system.

"I am sorry about that, ladies and gentlemen."

"We're not!" shouted most people.

"Now to get on with the sale, where were we?"

"We don't know and we don't care!"

As the General and his wife made their way towards the Flying Start to enjoy a celebratory drink the auction slowly got under way again through the hubbub of everyone talking about what they had just witnessed. They were enjoying their drinks at the bar when the two Japanese walked in.

"G'day, gents. I haven't seen you in here before, have I?"

"No, we are new here, we would like two double Scottish whiskies please."

At the sound of Takada's voice Chuck and Hetty Joy turned to see who the new patrons were and the General visibly stiffened, still unable to suppress those feelings ingrained in him during the war. It took some seconds before he nodded to the two Japanese in curt acknowledgement of their presence.

"Coming right up, hey doll, how about pouring a couple of large Scotches for these gentlemen? Are you here for the auction? Wait a minute, silly of me to ask, I mean we're all here for the auction, aren't we? Me and my missus came from Australia. We must be mad, eh?"

"We came from Japan."

"Well, I'd never have guessed if you hadn't told me."

Bill and his missus smiled, Takada smiled back at them.

"Look, I'm sorry guys, I didn't mean anything, but you sure do look Japanese."

"Yes, indeed we are, and not very happy Japanese either."

He and his friend held their glasses up to each other, said Campai and downed the neat whiskies.

"Oh?" said Bill to the two now slightly grimacing faces.

"Yes, we failed to buy the swords from our country just now. Can we have the same again please?"

"Didn't know there were any swords in the auction mate."

He looked at the crestfallen pair.

"So you really wanted them, eh?"

"Yes, but the Arab wanted them more. Twenty seven thousand British Pounds more."

"Wow! Twenty seven thousand? Wow! How many swords were there?"

"Eight."

"Were they worth that much?"

"Possibly just a little more and it would have been a matter of pride for us to have taken them back to Japan."

"Oh yeah, pride, yeah, I can see how it would. Well, if you're prepared to pay more I know what I'd do, I'd go straight up to Rawlston manor, where Sheikh Rattle and Roll is staying, make him a better offer and maybe you'd have a chance of buying them, especially if you give him the old Japanese honour thing. They say the Sheikh's a good guy so maybe you could still buy them."

"I do not think so."

The General cut in.

"He's right, take the fight to the enemy, you know, like in the war."

There was silence as Takada and his friend looked at him with suspicion.

"American?"

"Yeah."

"And doubtless in the war?"

"Yes, in the Pacific."

Takada nodded thoughtfully as they both sipped their whiskies and turned their gaze to the 38's behind the bar.

"Oh, but give it a go mate," Bill quickly picked up the conversation, "after all you've got nothing to lose, I mean if you really want something then sometimes you just have to go out there and get it, like I did with my missus here."

He put his arm around her to emphasise the point.

"Ah, yes, I see. You are right so we shall try. Could you direct us please to this Rawlston Manor?"

"It's the big house up on the hill, you can't miss it. Yeah, I'd go and appeal to the Sheikh's kind nature if I were you."

"Thank you, we will attempt this. Goodbye."

"Sayonara."

"Ah, Sayonara."

They bowed to the Australian couple and made to leave. In the doorway Takada turned back and looked at the General.

"We both fought in the war in the Pacific as well."

He stood there in silence.

"We lost."

He bowed to the General and walked out of the pub.

As they walked across the green the two Japanese talked about whether they really should go and see the Sheikh. Would they be losing face? No, they would not be going to beg, they would be going to attempt to succeed where they had so far failed. When they arrived at the manor sometime later the door was opened to them by one of the Arab bodyguards.

"We have come to speak with the Sheikh."

The one who was not the Religious One motioned them inside and disappeared into the lounge. Reappearing he ushered them forward. The Sheikh was slightly surprised at the sight of the two Japanese. Takada looked at the swords laid out on the table.

"To what do we owe this visit, my friends?"

"It is concerning the swords that you bought today. You see, I was the one bidding against you from the beginning. I wanted to buy them to take home to Japan, but you seemed so intent on purchasing them that I was forced to drop out."

"I see, well I really became most interested because somebody else wanted them and that told me they had value. There is nothing of interest in this auction for me so I simply decided to bid on the swords and you kindly established their value for me."

"You were not truly desirous of possessing them?"

"No, not really."

"Then I would like to make you a proposal. I am prepared to offer you more than you paid for them. I am sincere and would be honoured if we could agree a price so that we can take them back to Japan."

Takada was excited there was even a possibility.

"Nonsense! If they mean that much to you then you must accept them as a gift. I do not wish to make profit from such things. I give them to you as a present. I insist."

Takada's face fell and he looked at the floor.

"But I could not accept them for I lost them in the combat of the auction room and I must win them back with honour by giving of myself for them. I am sorry, but I cannot accept."

The Sheikh was most put out by this and consulted the Religious One. After a minute or two he said,

"This is indeed a problem. As an Arab I am pleased to make you a gift for it is our nature and custom. You understand that I do not want or need money for these swords and I understand that you seem to be unable to accept them as a gift. We must somehow make a compromise."

They were all thinking about how to make this compromise when Rawlston, the worse the wear for booze, arrived back at the manor. He breezed into the lounge whistling loudly, cock-a-hoop at the large amount of money he had made that day at the auction to find that his home now contained even more foreigners. The situation took some time to be explained to him, but as he came to grips with it he announced,

"Well I did keep one sword back, actually I forgot about it because it was in the library. I'll just go and get it."

The Sheikh looked at the two Japanese and shrugged. Rawlston came back carrying a lacquered box. Opening it he took the sword out and removed the brocade bag it was wrapped in.

"Here if you want it just pay me the equivalent of what the Sheikh paid for one of the others and it's yours."

He couldn't believe the amount of money that was flowing his way that day.

The two Japanese looked at the sword, but neither moved.

"I mean the Sheikh paid twenty seven thousand pounds plus 10% auctioneer's commission plus 14% VAT on the commission. So we just divide his total by eight and that's what you pay me for this one, OK?"

Again they did not move. They both seemed frozen.

"Alright I'll even knock the VAT off if it clinches the deal."

Only an extremely well-oiled Rawlston would make such an offer. Still they did not respond.

"Look, I know it's not as fancy as some of the others, but it is in its own box, so either you pay me the money or I'm going to keep it!" he said agitatedly as he thrust the sword roughly back into the box.

The Sheikh intervened.

"Do you have a problem? Is this sword no good?"

Takada looked at him.

"I will buy this sword for the agreed amount."

Straightaway his friend began to count pound notes into Rawlston's greedy hands.

"Very good, very good, then you are happy Mr.Rolton?"

"Oh yes, Sheikh, I'm happy alright."

Rawlston left them and went off into the back of the house, whistling his silly tune and counting his money. The Religious One lifted the sword from the box.

"Please!"

Takada's voice stopped the Arab just as he was about to unsheathe the blade.

"Please, may I?"

He bowed and gently took the sword.

"You see it just might be that this sword was not made for us to simply admire. In fact, in Japan, this might not be regarded as a sword at all."

The two Japanese carefully examined it and the look they exchanged after they had studied the handle was one almost of fear. They closed the box and placed the sword on top of it. Takada's friend knelt and began to pray.

"You see in my country the sword is sacred. The legend says that the islands of Japan were formed by drips of water that fell from the blade of a sword that had been dipped into the ocean. It became the favoured weapon of the Samurai and a great status symbol. To be Emperor of Japan you must possess three objects, the Jewel, the Mirror and the Sword."

He picked up one of the swords the Sheikh had bought.

"This longer one is Katana, the shorter one is Wakizashi, together they are Daisho, only worn by Samurai or higher rank. The Katana and Wakizashi you bought today are from the middle or early sixteen hundreds, in Edo period, except for two of them, one of which is not a proper sword and the other too modern. We examined them carefully. This one for example has beautifully carved bone mountings, but was made just before nineteen hundred for tourists. Proper Nihonto do not have such mountings. The blade of this will be soft, the true Nihonto blade is hard, so to us this is not a real sword. This other one has Arabic numerals stamped on the blade and was made for a non-commissioned officer in World War II. Neither have serious value. That leaves six swords that are quite good, three of them are Wakizashi which could be worn by everyone below Samurai such as craftsmen or merchants and they are in their plain wooden Saya, you say 'Scabbard', called Shira-Saya. They each have some value, but not to the amount you paid, which brings us to the last three."

The Sheikh was becoming slightly uneasy that the swords might actually prove to be worth very little. His concern was not the money, he simply did not want Rawlston to have gained even the slightest satisfaction from having tricked him.

"These three, as you can see from their Saya, are different. These Saya are beautifully made, polished with horsetail reed and lacquered. The fittings on these two swords in particular match each other, so they are Daisho and have good value. We removed the peg that holds the handle to the base of each of the swords and looked at the Mei, the signature of the maker hidden underneath. They are each by good and respected makers and so bring the value of your swords to a level a little above what you paid for them."

The Sheikh nodded sagely, as if he had known all along, but inside he was somewhat relieved.

"These swords are very fine and most certainly old, for as I have said we know the age from which they came and the people who made them. They are very good, of this there is no question and that is why we wanted to take them home with us."

Takada indicated the sword on top of the box and shook his head.

"But this, this may not be a sword at all."

"Not a sword? But we can all see that is precisely what it is."

"Physically you are right of course, for this sword is the longer type, called Tachi, that preceded Katana. But this sword's spiritual powers may greatly outweigh its physical ones. There is a possibility that in my country this could be seen as much, much more than a mere sword, for we think that this might be one of our most Sacred Spirits, a God in its own right. It is just possible that this could be Tenka-ichi! If indeed it is then in my country it would be feared and revered, worshipped and blessed and cared for as no other. It would be the rarest of the rare, finest of the fine, most powerful of the most powerful, most sought after of all the swords in the history of Japan and, if it is, it may only be unsheathed by one of the highest calling in our religion."

Takada glanced at his friend, now praying with eyes closed.

"I would be most proud to tell you the story of Tenka-ichi if you would like to hear it?"

The three Arabs most certainly wanted to know about this Spirit, this God of whom Takada had spoken. And so, as his friend prayed and the fire crackled in the hearth, Takada told them the story.

He told them of the dynasties, of the Samurai, of the wars and of the expertise that had developed so early in his country's history in the making of weapons. He took them back in time to when the sword was master of all, to the time when the highest military power in the land issued a command that a sword should be made that would forever be the embodiment of their souls and the creed they lived by. Throughout Japan a search that was to take two years was undertaken to locate the finest of blade makers. Once found he was commanded to create a blade that should be fired by their Gods, tempered by their Spirits, toughened by their Beliefs and honed by their Religion. It was to be a blade that would forever be embedded in their minds as the symbol of the very greatest power. A blade that would survive the centuries, that would be worshipped and revered and would be the envy of all men for all time. He was commanded to live at the most sacred of temples, to use any materials necessary and to develop his skills in whatever methods of manufacture he deemed appropriate to create such a sword.

Takada told them how the blade maker invoked the spirits to help him in his work as he toiled for five long years to develop a metal that was extremely strong and hard, that had an appearance and lustre different from all other metals and that could be worked into a blade that would hold its edge for an eternity. How he developed the tempering of the metal and the eradication of impurities that could create any weakness. How he covered the blade with clay except for the cutting edge so that, when fired and quenched with water, this edge became hardened to an extreme that, together with its curve, would allow the sword to cut through flesh, bone and even armour.

He told them of the great lengths the blade maker went to in polishing the blade, the different kinds of stones he used and the different angles he polished at so that at the end of his labour the shine on the blade would last for a hundred years or more.

How it had been commanded that should it become necessary to sharpen the blade it must only ever be done using crushed sea shells. How legend said that the handle had been made from the spike of a Narwhal, turned and fashioned and carrying a golden Kiku-mon, the chrysanthemum emblem of royalty, but how in reality it was known that the handle was but a simple one with the emblem delicately carved into it. How the first blood the blade was reputed to have drawn was the blood of the blade maker himself by his own hand at the command of the highest religious being. With his death its method of manufacture was lost for all time and its uniqueness preserved.

All the people revered Tenka-ichi, meaning 'First Under Heaven'. In times of crisis they prayed to it, in good times they brought presents to honour it and in both good times and bad they made sacrifices to it. It had truly become a god in its own right when it was tragically lost in one of the greatest battles of the 'Hundred Years War' and was never seen again. Only drawings of it remained. With its loss there came a great pestilence upon the land, bringing famine and death. The people searched everywhere for Tenka-ichi, but it had vanished, lost to their world forever.

"It was the sight of the carving of the sixteen petal Kiku-mon on the outside of the lacquered box that initially shocked us. We must examine the Mei on this sword for we both know the sign of this most legendary of blade makers from the holy writings. My friend here has studied Tenka-ichi all his life. His father was a sword maker and told him stories about it from when he was young, so you could say he is something of an expert in this matter."

As Takada finished speaking his friend, still kneeling in prayer, lifted the sword and began to remove the peg that held the handle to it. At first it seemed to be stuck, but then it was eased out and he gently disassembled the handle. They looked at the part of the sword the handle had encompassed. It was covered in a light, black rust, an indication of great age. There was no mark on the side they were looking at so they turned the sword over. Suddenly they both exclaimed loudly and began to visibly shake. Whilst his friend steadied himself to rebuild the handle Takada held himself in a permanent bow to the sword, mopped his face with his handkerchief and nodded to the Sheikh.

"It is the signature of the master, Amakuni! This is Tenka-ichi!"

The Arabs were spellbound by the mixture of fear and respect affecting the two Japanese and looked on as Takada's friend, now praying loudly, bowed to the sword and ever so slowly began to withdraw the blade. As he did so a sudden burst of wind came rattling at the windows, making the fire burn brightly in the draft and dance flickering reflections of silver tinged with blue mixed with a deep golden lustre from the sword into their eyes.

Tenka-ichi was there, as complete and perfect as it had been made all those centuries ago, still a Spirit, still a God whose presence they could feel as the wind moaned its pressure at the windows making the flames hungrily consume the logs that sparked and crackled in the hearth.

They stared as Tenka-ichi was turned in a slow, delicate movement for their inspection. Then Takada's friend, still praying loudly, slowly re-sheathed the blade, painstakingly wrapped the sword in its brocade bag and placed it

107

reverently back into the box. There was no wind now, the quiet of the old manor house only gently disturbed by the burning logs.

"I am such a lucky man," said the Sheikh quietly, "to be here in this place with you my friends and with this, this god of yours. Allah has brought us here. His purpose is not always clear, but I believe that we are meant to come to such places and meet people such as you and share in your experiences as together we travel the great journey of life. I am most grateful to you for recounting to us this tale of your Tenka-ichi, but I now feel even more strongly that it is you who must take the swords that I have purchased back to Japan."

Takada though was still faced with the same problem.

It was the Religious One who came up with the idea.

"Perhaps my Lord, to overcome any difficulty we could take the swords to Japan and present them ourselves?"

The Sheikh truly hoped this proposal would be found acceptable.

"Tell me, I understand that you have racehorses in Japan?"

"This is so."

"If we came to your country would you help us to investigate such horses?"

"Of course, it would be my honour to arrange this for you."

"And if we were then to present these swords to whoever you wish, this would get us out of our little problem?"

"Yes indeed."

"Splendid! It is settled then. But I do have one question that I would very much like to know the answer to. Pray tell me what might be the value of this Tenka-ichi?"

Takada shook his head.

"It has no value."

"No value? But surely it has great value?"

"What I mean is that neither you or I could place a value upon it. I believe that, were the highest religious being in Japan aware of its existence there is no amount of money in our country that would not be offered to reclaim it."

The Sheikh raised his eyebrows in astonishment.

"But you, you have just bought it from that ridiculous man for..."

"A little under four thousand British Pounds."

"You mean to say that your religious people would have paid him a great deal more?"

"Tens of millions of Yen, perhaps hundreds of millions, without question."

"And you, if you would tell us, what will you be paid for it?"

Takada shook his head again.

"Nothing. We will present it to those who should have been watching over it and we will take no payment. Ours will be the honour for all time. Our lives will be remembered for finding and bringing home Tenka-ichi, for us this will be payment enough."

This appealed immensely to the Sheikh.

He was so amused by the fact that Rawlston had done himself out of such vast riches that he was soon laughing about this gross error of judgement together with his two body guards. Even the normally reserved Japanese were grinning from ear to ear and their combined laughter filled the room. On hearing the noise Rawlston came back into the lounge, upon which the Sheikh began to laugh uncontrollably and collapsed onto the floor clutching at his side.

To make matters worse the two Japanese bowed to Rawlston, eliciting howls of glee from the Sheikh and making him hammer his fist on the floor in pure delight at Rawlston's total ignorance of what he had just done and his look of complete bemusement at their hysterics.

"You're all mad bastards, you bloody foreigners!" he shouted and stomped off down the hall to his room, leaving their shrieks of laughter echoing around the manor.

Day Five

Friday brought the Little Saddlington Beer Drinking Contest, which had attracted no less than eighty two entrants who all reckoned they could down three pints of beer faster than Bill Boyd. Fifty seven of those who wished to participate were men and seven of the MP's were among the twenty five women. Each person had contributed the five pounds that Bill had asked for, making a total of four hundred and ten pounds as the prize for the winner.

It was a feat of organisation just pouring the necessary two hundred and forty six pints and laying them out on the trestle tables. With so many participants the only way to check when each had finished was to appoint a number of referees who were standing on the benches at regular intervals and included the policeman, the butcher, the vicar, the Scotsman, the Cornishman and the Lancashire Lads.

It had been decided that the twelve people who finished first would go into the grand final to be held two hours later. A local teacher fired a starting pistol to begin the competition and the host of pints began to vanish. Bill Boyd consumed his with relish, but was startled to find that the referees had determined that one or two others had run him close.

He was not the only one who belched after his beer this time.

The animal pens contained two bulls, four heifers, nine cows with a number of calves and almost a hundred sheep comprised of lambs, ewes and rams. Twelve sows, many of them with litters, were kept in separate pig pens from the seven boars that had been put up for sale and there were also large quantities of chickens that were making one dickens of a chicken noise from their wooden coops stacked in a line down the side of the pens.

Farmers clustered around the animals and sheepdogs clung to their master's heels as they weaved their way from pen to pen, meeting old friends and talking about the quality of what was on offer. The pressure from the amount of people in the crowd was becoming acute as Shipley, microphone in hand, walked to the window to address them.

"Ladies and gentlemen we now come to the livestock that we have for sale today, all on view in the pens at the side of the hall as you can see and I'm sure you'll agree that it's a pretty good selection."

Shipley's voice was cracking as he spoke, the honey and lemon drink seemed no longer to be helping.

"As you've had plenty of time to make your choices we'll start with lot number two thousand two hundred and seventy six which is the first of the two bulls. Now then, who will open the bidding?"

It was Herpes who started the trouble, ably assisted by the Sheepdog and the Labrador.

The 'Erp was still a bit cheesed off by that business down at the river as well as having all these strange dogs suddenly invade his territory and had been looking to reassert himself as King of Little Saddlington.

He took an instant dislike to these two and typically having picked two of the toughest dogs present launched himself into a savage attack upon them. In the heat of their snarling, biting fight they crossed under the rails and into the pen that held the huge Charolais bull that Shipley was trying to sell. The bull had been a perfectly placid animal until that moment, but three fighting, barking dogs entering the close domain of a bull is a recipe for disaster and it was a disaster that happened next as the bull began crashing around in his pen, trying to get at the dogs who were now spilling their desperate fight over into the next pen, which was full of sheep.

"Mind that bull!" shouted Shipley and, for almost the first time since the start of the auction four days previously, he suddenly had absolutely everyone's attention. However the bull's attention was firmly fixed on the three fighting dogs and in a shattering blow of solid muscle he demolished the entire side of his pen and began to chase after the three of them as they fought on, seemingly oblivious to the angry hulk that was bearing down upon them.

"Look out! The bull's loose!"

Shipley could not have shouted anything worse had he tried as, with every person in Little Saddlington echoing his words, the crowd panicked and people began pushing each other as they tried to get away from the area of the pens. To assist matters a large number of sheep ran out through the bull's now non-existent pen into the terrified throng whilst the bull began demolishing some more railed pen fencing that the three dogs had just vanished through.

The pens had been reasonably strongly built but hardly to withstand the full force of an enraged bull. With just one short shoulder charge most of the pen wall gave way, the bull lowered his head, caught part of the remaining pen rails with one of his horns and lifted them high into the air. Ripping the side off four pens at once the angry Charolais went stamping through into the central pen area with rails cascading around him. As pigs and more sheep mixed with some of the cows and their calves and began to panic as much as the crowds the three dogs fought their way into the passageway between the pens, straight into more dogs who instantly joined the fray. Pen gates gave way as the crowd crushed against them and suddenly a whole host of farm animals were on the loose being chased by all kinds of dogs and together they charged through the crowd into the square.

The second bull, a big Hereford, simply walked out of his newly opened pen and proceeded around the back of the hall and down the other side of it, heading off people who were running in that direction.

The irate Charolais pursued the fighting dogs and careered out towards the square bringing down more than a dozen chicken coops as he went and feathers began to fly as squawking chickens sped about through the panicking crowds.

Screaming people ran in all directions as the huge Charolais and Hereford bulls both rampaged into the square from either side of the village hall and chickens, sheep, pigs, cows and people stampeded for their lives. Shipley could only look on in abject horror at the scene of pandemonium and devastation below him. There was not a hope of anyone bringing the situation under control as the animals fragmented out through the people in the square and onto the village green, where the final of the Little Saddlington Beer Drinking Contest was just getting under way.

Bill Boyd and the eleven other finalists were facing each other down either side of two trestle tables and six referees were ready to scrupulously monitor them. The starting gun fired and they picked up their pints and began to drink. Bill was standing opposite Long Tall Sally and found that her eyes were most disconcertingly looking straight into his. The crowd roared encouragement as they both put their empty second pints down at exactly the same moment. With the crowd screaming at them she kept looking straight at him and started to down the third, delighted to see his eyes opening wide in disbelief as her glass began to tilt upward faster than his. He even pointed at her across the table as he struggled with his pint and the noise became deafening as the crowd urged her on.

But Bill Boyd was no longer trying to beat Long Tall Sally, nor was he pointing at her and nor were the crowds shouting encouragement, for it was a rapidly approaching Charolais bull, attracted by her bright, power red shirt, that was causing all of these things to happen. Bill didn't want to lose the contest, but, as the bull accelerated towards LT and she threw her empty glass down and yelled at her victory, he threw his own glass aside, reached across the table and pulled her straight over it and down on top of him. Whilst she kept loudly proclaiming that she had won along with her surprise at Bill's impulsiveness, the bull reached the table behind her and Bill, now terrified they were going to be trampled, pointed at it behind her back.

"Bull!" he shouted.

"No, it's true, I won and you know it!" yelled LT sitting astride him and beginning to pummel him in friendly manner.

"Bull! Bull! Bull!" he yelled, still pointing at the animal as it towered over the table and the two of them.

"True! True! True!" she yelled back, but it did begin to dawn on her that the look on Bill's face just might not be one of play. As she realised that everything was not quite right the bull gave out a loud snorting sound.

"Bull?" squeaked Bill and Long Tall Sally slowly turned to find that Bill's identification of what was standing immediately behind her was one hundred percent correct. She screamed, leapt off him and sprinted for cover. Bill, now lying there on his back facing the bull, screamed himself, however the giant Charolais had lost interest now the object that had originally caught its attention was gone and so, as Bill Boyd lay there with his eyes shut tight, praying for deliverance, the bull turned and ambled away.

As people ran for their lives there seemed to be no end to the stampede, however the Little Saddlington Great Escape finally began to come under control through one surprising incident. It was one of the heifer's who started to put an end to the pandemonium when she came face to face with the disgruntled Charolais as he snorted his way across the green. Whether the bull had forgotten about the dogs or not his interest immediately shifted straight to the heifer and he stopped dead in his tracks to look at her. It wouldn't have been so bad if he'd just stayed looking at her, but no, being a full blooded bull who had been confined to his pen for far too long, right there in the middle of the green with people covering their children's eyes everywhere around them, the bull mounted the heifer.

On that day more questions about what the animals were doing were asked by youngsters of their parents than possibly on any day in history. But at least this lovemaking allowed some of the farmers to get ropes around the two animal's necks. Once the conjugating was finished the bull seemed to be tired, or at least satisfied enough that they were able to lead him back to the pens, which were being swiftly rebuilt by a small army. All in all it took well over an hour to get everything under control, but although at the end of it most of the animals had been herded back into the pens, the Hereford bull was still happily progressing his way down the valley, resisting every attempt to stop him. Some of the chickens weren't caught for days, but all the other animals were rounded up, unfortunately not before the rams had administered some nasty butts to a number of people.

Sadly there were some injuries, although happily none were too serious, and the MP's tended to them whilst Shipley apologised to everyone over the PA system and Charles helped the farmers reorganise the pens. Whether any of the pen fittings had been loosened by some devious person prior to the Little Saddlington Great Escape was hard to say, but it was a distinct possibility as the Charolais had certainly made short work of them. In the end two hours had been lost before Shipley could restart the auction despite the continued absence of the Hereford bull which seemed hell bent on leaving the county or the country.

The Major's cottage was bare now with only the very last of the possessions he wanted to take with him remaining. These he could only move on the Saturday morning as the auction house removal van was not available before then. On that Friday, having nowhere else to stay, he had made a train journey of two and a half hours and then a taxi ride of some fifteen minutes before finally arriving to spend the night at his future home.

He was met at the door of the home for ex-services people by a rotund and formidable looking nurse who brusquely introduced herself as 'Sister'.

Entering the ominous looking grey building he found the hallway and lounges that adjoined it crowded with elderly people. Sister strode on, not even offering to help him with his cases, and began to climb the stairs.

"We have a lift, but we don't like you to use it as it saves us electricity."

Along a dingy, dirty corridor he followed her and together they entered a room at the far end of it. Sister switched on the light and opened the curtains. It was still dim in the room. Out of the window all that could be seen was the grey wall of an adjoining building with a little sky above. She showed him the wash basin, the cupboard, the bed and the separate toilet and bathroom along the corridor that had to be shared with others. She said that he would be just in time for lunch if he hurried and left him standing in the cold, stark room that was to be his future home.

The bed was like an old hospital bed, having a curved tubular metal headboard with vertical bars and the bed springs, what there were of them, grated when he sat on the thin mattress. The room had a bare wooden floor and there was only the one naked central light bulb. There was a musty smell and the Major tried to open the window to let some fresh air in, but it was jammed shut. He stared out of it. No river, no trees, no hills, no vibrant living nature to immerse himself in, no runs of salmon forging their way upstream, no feeling of homeliness, friendliness or warmth, just cold unfeeling grey stone staring back at him. He felt a strange, shuddering spasm, as if death were close by, watching him, waiting. Quickly he took off his coat, washed his hands and face and went downstairs.

Throughout lunch he talked to the other residents. To his mind they were old and he wasn't. They were a lonely, sickly bunch trying to get by in a place of no hope. They talked about the war and found out each other's service and rank. The food, a kind of tasteless stodge, reminded him of school food. An elderly man died in one of the lounges while they ate. The doctor arrived in minutes and, after his examination, Sister and her assistants swiftly removed the body to a room somewhere at the back of the building to await the undertakers. After lunch the Major inspected the home. There wasn't much to see, just three lounges and a conservatory at the front where the residents fought each other to get a seat in a bit of light. That was it, just these three rooms and his bedroom.

"Sister, if I want to walk to the shops, which way do I go?" he asked her.

"Now we don't want you making trouble, whatever you want you give us the money and we get it whenever one of us goes shopping. You might fall over and hurt yourself out there. We can't allow that to happen, now can we?"

"But what if I want to go for a walk?"

"A walk? Whatever for? Well one of the staff will have to go with you, but we don't encourage people to go for walks as it takes us away from our duties. We prefer if you just walk around the home and then we're close at hand if you get into trouble."

Trouble? What trouble could he possibly get into? He walked miles every day up and down the river fishing his big fly rod for hours at a time and considered himself perfectly fit for a man of his age. Walk round the home? What nonsense.

"What about if I want to have some visitors?"

"Visitors? We don't really think it's on for you to have visitors. How would it be if every resident had visitors? We'd be swamped. Anyway most people are glad to leave their elderly family with us, after which they don't get any visitors."

But the Major had a number of friends in Little Saddlington who might want to come and see him once in a while. He tried again.

"But I have friends who will want to visit me, you're surely going to allow me to see them, aren't you?"

"Oh I see, we're going to be difficult are we? Well I've told you what we think of your having visitors and you'll have to abide by the rules if you want to stay here."

That night he lay on his bed and thought about his life.

This would surely be the end of it for he knew he wouldn't last long once he came to this appalling place, nor would he want to. He woke in the early hours screaming Margaret's name as the screams from his men engulfed and overwhelmed him once more. The night nurse came and chastised him for waking some of the residents, saying they would have to administer sedatives to him every night if this was how he was going to behave. When she had gone he lay in the dark, listening to someone coughing in the next room and thinking about the only possible relief there was to end the miserable prospect of having to spend the rest of his life in this dreadful place.

His service revolver in the brass bound chest back at the cottage.

The Great Day

The Crow that was a Rook hung his head as he perched on the chimney pot and endured the monster tongue lashing his wife was giving him. The scolding went on and on, nothing he did was ever good enough for her. She blamed him for everything, the nesting sites he had selected, the building materials he had brought her, the weather and everything that was wrong with her life, which was a lot.

This had been going on for weeks. Two aborted attempts at nest building had tired him and made her even more unbearably irritable. Berating him about how late they were with finishing the nest she gave him one final broadside of abuse and sent him off to find more materials to build with.

Being only able to take so much he was now coming to the end of his tether. This sort of thing would never have happened back at the Rookery where you could simply use last year's nest, give it a bit of a spring clean, add a few twigs here and there and you had a brand new nest. Why he had ever married this most unpleasant of birds who he could never satisfy was beyond him. It wasn't as if they were even going to have any kids as building a nest was the only part of his matrimonial rights she would allow him to enjoy.

He was flying across the pasture towards the wood when something in the hedge caught his eye. He turned and swooped down to have a look at it. There, all but hidden in the middle of the hedge, was an old nest. He couldn't believe his luck. It was perfect. All he had to do was get it out of the hedge and back to the chimney and his wife would never have anything to complain about again.

Get it back, yes, but how?

It was embedded in the hedge and looked as if it was too large for him to carry. He would just have to break it up and carry it back piece by piece. He began plucking at the hedge to make a hole in the foliage large enough to be able to get at it and as he worked he carefully inspected the nest, finding it to be well made with the fibres bound in tight. He became even more desperate to take it back. After almost three hours of working he started to pull it from the centre of the hedge and eventually managed to get it right to the edge of the hole he had made.

'Now then,' he thought to himself, 'this is so well made it would be a shame to break it up, but how on earth am I going to be able to fly with it?'

However so great was his determination to take it back in one piece and show his wife that he really was capable of getting things right, he conjured up a most daring plan.

It was the lieutenant of the MP's, Dolores, who sought out the General early on that Saturday morning and conveyed the communication to him that had been received from headquarters. This was the result of the General's enquiries that had started way back in Reno with young John and which had led him to ask the MP's base commander to help in the search for some final critical details. He listened as she outlined the information, then she saluted and went about her business and the General determined that it was high time he finally went about his.

In the village hall a smart looking man dressed in a bright orange tweed jacket, waistcoat and matching plus two's was making his way to his seat followed by his strange looking dog. On the man's head was a flat cap in matching tweed and gold rimmed glasses rested on his nose as he opened his catalogue and the dog lay down under his feet. He had decided that it would be safe to come to the village hall for this last day and that, if he was going to do so, he ought to be dressed fit for the part, even if he did not intend to buy anything.

He was clean shaven, smart and businesslike as he perused his catalogue. One or two people thought there was something strangely familiar about him. But such was the dramatic change they were all completely fooled.

It was Bob and Herpes.

At around the same time Rawlston pulled his car up just short of a group of three MP's as the tallest one held the palm of her white gloved hand up to stop him.

"Get out of the bloody way, will you?" he shouted at them, sticking his head out of the window. The tall one walked around to the side of the vehicle and looked at him.

"No parking beyond this point today, bud. The village is too busy already so you'll have to park here and walk."

"Walk! Do you know who I am? Bloody walk! I most certainly will not! I'm on the list so get out of the way!"

"Listen buster, the list is no longer operational and none of us are moving from here so this is as far as you're going. Do you understand?"

"Who the bloody hell do you think you are? You've got no jurisdiction here! Tell those two idiots to get out of the way before I run them over!"

Rawlston revved up the engine with the result that the tall MP reached in, grabbed the ignition key, turned the engine off and smartly yanked the keys out of the car. Rawlston lost his temper and leapt out, hurling insults.

"Give me back those keys you stupid bitch! I'm driving through to the village hall whether you like it or not! Now give me those bloody keys!"

The three MP's looked at each other.

"Guess there's only one answer for Mr.Important here," said one of them and, as the tall one's arm went back she shouted,

"The pitcher's on the mound! Will it be a curve ball? Will it be a slider? Oh no! Here comes the fast ball!"

With that the MP's arm shot forward and Rawlston could only watch in horror as his car keys were launched high into the air up and over the green verge and the small hedge at the side of the road to land with a splash somewhere out in the river.

"Guess you'll be parking here after all, buster!"

"You stupid bloody American cow! You're all stupid bloody American cows!"

The two standing at the front of the car began to slowly walk around towards Rawlston and now there was a distinctly hard look about them.

Sometime later the Sheikh and his men were leaving the manor when they ran into Rawlston on the doorstep.

"Ah, Mr.Rolton, such a splendid day and this day we shall sign the sale of your estate to me, yes?"

Rawlston just stood there looking at them.

"But you are all wet Mr.Rolton! Have you been swimming?"

"Huh!" grunted Rawlston and squelched off down the hall.

The Major was taking the early morning train back to Little Saddlington.

He sat grim faced in his compartment gazing out of the window not seeing the passing landscape, his mind firmly gripped by the thought of committing that most terrible of deeds, the taking of his own life. He had exhausted every possibility in trying to find a new home and the awful place he had just left was the only one he could afford. He knew there was nothing else for it now but to complete the act Rawlston had interrupted that night at the cottage. For the Major time stood still as the train rumbled on, taking him inexorably towards his end.

He had arranged with Charles that he would meet the auction house removal van at the cottage at 11.30a.m. and he arrived there at about a quarter past. He couldn't open the front door, being unable to get the key to fit into the lock, which he found most odd. He went around to the back door only to find the same thing happened. With his mind filled with the notion of leaving this earth he could make no sense of it and tried to open the front door again.

He was still trying when the removal van arrived.

"Major! Major!"

He turned to the van driver.

"All of your stuff's gone, we took it to the auction ages ago."

"What? What do you mean you 'took it to the auction'?"

"We got orders to take it all to the auction first thing this morning, so that's what we did."

"Orders to take my belongings? Don't be ridiculous! You're supposed to be helping me move everything to my new home!"

"I know Major and I feel right bad about it, but he said we had to do it. We've emptied the cottage and he's changed the locks on the doors."

"Changed the locks?"

"I'm sorry Major, but what could we do? Mr.Shipley agreed with him and he is our boss you know."

"What the hell are you talking about, man? You can't just take my things and put them in the auction, that's everything I own! What about the fish? I want to present it to the pub today before I leave. What the hell do you think you're doing?"

"Now Major, please don't go losing your temper with us. The fish has gone into the auction as well. I'm sorry but we were only doing what we were told and you know Mr.Rawlston can be a very difficult man to deal with."

A burning sea of red hot rage came sweeping through George Roberts.

"Rawlston! That bloody man! Rawlston! I'll kill him!"

Without so much as another word to the worried van driver he set off at pace towards the village. People he passed on the way wished him 'good morning', but they were ignored and some were rudely pushed out of the way as he approached the green. Entering the marquee he shouldered his way through those inside and spied Charles.

"Montgomery!"

"Good morning, Major. What can I do for you?"

"Where are my belongings Montgomery?"

"You're belongings, Major? I think they were all sold on Wednesday."

"No, not those belongings, all the things Rawlston stole from my cottage this morning and entered into the auction!"

"Stole?"

"Yes! Stole! Have you seen him this morning?"

"Mr.Rawlston?"

"Yes of course Mr.Rawlston! For heaven's sake stop gibbering will you?"

"Well I think he's in Mr.Shipley's back office in the hall, Major."

"Oh he is, is he? Now just you get my things back right away."

"I'll get hold of Mr.Shipley at once, Major."

However with the sale well under way the field telephone was in constant use relaying the bidding from the marquee to the hall. As the Major ran out of patience Charles waited his chance and grabbed the telephone at the first opportunity, but Shipley did not want to know about the Major's problem and shouted down the phone that Charles was not to bother him again. Charles turned back apologetically only to find the Major had disappeared.

George Roberts hunted up and down the rows of tables until he came across his old, brass bound chest under one of them. He took the brass key from his pocket and unlocked it. Reaching inside under his uniform he grabbed the revolver and, hiding it under his jacket, made to leave the marquee.

The General hailed him from across the sea of people, but the Major seemed not to hear and kept going. From the crazed look on the Major's face Chuck Verbeer could see that something was very wrong and began to push through the crowd himself and follow as the Major made straight for the village hall. Outside the hall the General spied Bert Hughes and waved to him shouting,

"Something's up with the Major, Bert, let's go!"

The two of them entered the hall and forced their way through the mass of people. Bert managed to spy the Major, who was making slow progress towards the far end of the hall, but as the two of them neared him he slipped through the crowd and disappeared towards the back office.

The Sheikh was sitting at the office desk looking over some documents when the Major burst in. Before his startled men could move to stop him he had the revolver out and pointed at Rawlston.

"Steal my things would you? This time I'll make sure the world is rid of you, you bloody little scumbag!"

Rawlston jumped like a startled rabbit, his solicitor dived for cover, the two Arab bodyguards were halfway around the table and the Major had clicked the hammer back on the revolver when a powerful hand suddenly engulfed his and another applied a painful, vicelike grip to his arm. Finding himself unable to even pull the trigger and the gun being forcefully pointed away from Rawlston and up at the ceiling, the Major heard Chuck Verbeer's voice,

"Well done, George! Well done! It's all over now, just relax, there's a good man."

It was the Major's turn to be shocked as his friend calmly but powerfully forced the revolver from his grip. Even the General's smiling face couldn't stop the Major being overwhelmed with frustration at having failed to kill Rawlston and he made a sort of choking sound of despair as he slumped, defeated, over the corner of the desk from where Bert Hughes gently guided him back into the only available chair.

"I'll sue you, you old bastard!" yelled Rawlston, "Sergeant Hughes, you saw that! He tried to kill me! Arrest the silly old bugger for attempted murder!"

"It's all over now, gentlemen," said the General, "please sit down and carry on with what you were doing. The Major here just got a little excited, that's all."

He let the revolver drop to his side and looked at the two Arabs, standing there with daggers drawn. The Sheikh lifted his hand and they resumed their position at his side.

"That's better. Now then, would you please be so kind as to close and lock the door, Sergeant Hughes?"

The door closed behind him and the lock turned as the General raised the revolver and once more Rawlston found himself looking down the barrel. Immediately the two Arabs began to unsheathe their daggers again, but the General simply 'tut-tutted' them.

"Surely you boys know that one of these beats two of those?"

The Sheikh lifted his hand again.

"What the hell d'you think you're doing?" shouted Rawlston.

"If I were you Mr.Rawlston I'd be keeping real quiet. You see I practice with weapons like this every day, but even with all that practice this gun could still go off accidentally and, were that to happen right now, it would blow a hole straight through your head, right between your eyes."

The voice had changed and now held an icy tone, the face too had changed to a hardened mask of granite. Rawlston slowly sank back into his chair.

"Sheikh if you'll bear with me I would like to ask the Major here a question."

"Of course, please do."

The Sheikh if at first alarmed by these goings on was now most intrigued.

"Tell me, George, does the name 'Firefly' mean anything to you?"

The Major did not respond, he just sat there in a daze looking at the floor.

"Major Roberts!"

The Major's head snapped upright.

"I'm asking if you recognise the name 'Firefly'."

"Firefly? Well it seems a bit familiar Chuck...but I can't really remember."

"Think back to North Africa , George."

"North Africa? Firefly? Oh yes, of course, it was the name of a tank, wasn't it? One of your Shermans with a ruddy great gun on it if I'm not mistaken."

"Indeed it was, George, indeed it was. The gun was a seventeen pounder, but is that the only thing you can remember about the name?"

"Yes. Yes I think so, old boy. What on earth are you on about?"

"Logistics, George, just those bloody logistics we talked about, like those that weren't available to you at Wadi-el-Jabrin. Oh yes, I checked out your little escapade down there while I was making my enquiries. You know, I never would have found out about those logistical problems you British suffered had the same thing not happened to me in a different theatre of war, so with your indulgence, gentlemen, I'm going to tell you all a true war story."

No one had the slightest intention of trying to stop the General, after all it was he who was holding the gun.

"In 1942 and '43 British logistics in North Africa suffered a series of shortages. In the chaos of running from Rommel, then attacking him, then running, then attacking him again no one thought too much of a fuel shortage here, a medical or ammunition shortage there, nor even the odd food and water shortage for the troops at the front. In fact no one was to blame that these shortages were not looked into.

Not until the Battle of the Bulge where we too suffered shortages with logistics unable to supply us what we needed and where we needed it did I even get suspicious myself. Logistics, as you know George are run by people, most of whom are honest, but some of whom, unfortunately, are not. As I said before you are quite right, the name 'Firefly' was indeed the name given to one of our Shermans, but it was also used as a codename in North Africa, a codename for the person who was siphoning off critical supplies and selling them, sometimes even to the enemy, wherever he could just as long as he got his money."

The General paused, the room was silent.

"When we started our investigations late on in the war it was painfully slow. There was so much happening as we pushed through Germany and the chaos of the war ending covered a lot of the tracks that we were investigating. Anyway we were wrongly looking at our own logistical support where we thought the problem lay, when we should really have been looking at the British side. After the war as our people sorted and searched through countless records a large operation doing exactly what I have just described was uncovered. We traced this criminal network back to the British and then found that some of our own people had been working in collusion with it. Many of those involved were caught, but never the man at the top, never the man who organised the stealing from his own forces resulting in weakening them with shortages that left good men like George here stranded out in the desert, out of fuel and at the mercy of Rommel's troops. No, we never got the man known in North Africa as 'Firefly'."

The General still had the gun trained on Rawlston.

"Tell me something, Mr.Rawlston, what did you do in the war?"

"What do you mean? Why, I was in the Sappers!"

"No, you definitely were not in the Royal Engineers, although you did see service alright. First you were in North Africa, but your name wasn't Rawlston then, was it? Not when you became a Regimental Quartermaster in charge of supplies after the British beat the Italians in '41, just before Rommel came at them. Your name wasn't Rawlston then, but we both know your codename, don't we?"

"You're completely mad! Codename? Logistics? You've gone cuckoo in the head, man!"

"Oh there's no need to concern yourself about my sanity, but I must say it was a little strange that there I was sitting in my home in Nevada when I happened to read a newspaper advertisement for this auction, an advertisement that made me just have to come and find out. In all these years you never made a mistake until that advertisement. You covered your tracks and vanished, even though a lot of us were looking for you and my bet is you thought we'd given up, but you were wrong.

You see, gentlemen, 'Firefly' was the codename used by our traitor in North Africa, but when he was transferred to the European conflict with promotion to Division Deputy Quartermaster General he thoughtfully changed that codename to the one I read when I was sitting in my home in Reno. The one that made me just have to come and find out for myself, in case it really was him."

Still the silence lay heavy on the room, no one seemed to breathe as the General looked along the barrel of the revolver and into Rawlston's eyes.

"The codename that 'Firefly' was changed to, Mr.Rawlston, was 'Rubicon'!"

Sweat began trickling down the side of Rawlston's reddening face as they all looked at him.

"Utter rubbish! Total stupidity! You can't prove any of this! Why, I wasn't even in North Africa! You've got nothing on me! Nothing!"

"On the contrary, we've got everything on you, names, dates, codes, supply movements, even details of some of the payments you received. George, let me ask you another question. Have you ever heard of 'LAOS'?"

"Country in South East Asia, isn't it?"

"Indeed it is, it is also the initials of an American organisation that now spans the globe. LAOS stands for 'Looking After Our Soldiers'. We formed it after Vietnam when we found our country turned its back on so many who had fought for it at the very moment they needed its help. LAOS is funded by those ex-service people who became financially successful to help look after those who did not, whichever war they might have fought in, and through it a vast amount of military information and testimony is available. We have book, chapter and verse on your so called 'Mr.Rawlston' here and so, after his having gotten away with his crimes for all these years, we've finally caught up with him. For you 'Rawlston' the game is definitely over."

"But I am buying Mr.Rolton's estate for one million British pounds, are you saying it is not his to sell?"

The General, the Major and the Sergeant were staggered.

"It's his alright, Sheikh, bought with money gained through his deceit, money tainted with the blood of decent men."

"But it is not yet done, for some reason Mr.Rolton is very particular that I must wait until twelve o'clock before I sign the papers."

"Probably because midday is when he gets my cottage and the fishing back and then the estate will be complete with no loose ends. It's all over, Chuck, I've got to raise twenty five thousand pounds to get a new lease on the cottage and the fishing by twelve o'clock."

"Yes! And that gives Monty's Major here just three and a half minutes! Let's see how you get out of this one you old bastard!"

Rawlston's voice overflowed with venom as he saw his chance to divert their attention.

"But I can give you twenty five thousand pounds immediately," the Sheikh announced proudly.

"So can my people at LAOS," said the General.

"Oh, no you don't! I don't know what's going on here between you bastards, but the money has to come from Monty's Major, not from any third party. I have the right to determine that it really is the Major's money and I can refuse it if I think it's anyone else's! Can't I?"

With desperation creeping into his voice Rawlston turned to his lawyer.

"Yes, that is correct. It's written in the lease renewal clause that Mr.Rawlston is allowed to verify that any premium paid for the lease is the Major's own money and that it has not been put up by a third party. This was done originally to make sure that whoever occupied the cottage was a properly solvent person who would be fully capable of paying the rent."

"Let's face it, Chuck, he's beaten me. In a couple of minutes he'll have the cottage and the fishing back. He even removed the remainder of my belongings from the cottage this morning and put them in the auction just to spite me."

"What?"

"I've lost everything that was dear to me, it's a pretty comprehensive win I'm afraid."

"You mean you've got stuff in the auction?"

"Yes old boy, unfortunately, all the personal things I had intended to keep, everything I had in the world in fact."

"Which lot numbers are they George?"

"I don't know, I was more interested in trying to kill Rawlston than worry about lot numbers."

The General and the Sheikh looked at each other, both were thinking the same thing. Chuck Verbeer turned to the policeman as the Sheikh jumped to his feet.

"Bert, you're in charge of this until we get back, d'you want the gun?"

"Oh I doubt that'll be necessary General."

He looked at Rawlston.

"Sergeant Bert Hughes, Royal Engineers. France, Belgium, Holland, Germany. Now I really was in the Sappers and if I were you Mr.Rawlston I'd be keeping extremely quiet before I get myself into some really serious, physical trouble."

Together the Sheikh and the General rushed out of the office and into the hall as Shipley's voice warbled,

"Lot number two thousand eight hundred and thirty four..."

"Hold it! Hold everything right there!" shouted the General.

"Yes, hold all things!" shouted the Sheikh.

"Oh, for heaven's sake! What on earth is it now?"

The General sprang onto the stage and crossed to Shipley.

"What lot number are you on?"

"I just said it, two thousand eight hundred and thirty four! You're out of order! You shouldn't be up here!"

The General raised the revolver, bringing a shriek from those in the hall, and placed the end of the barrel against Shipley's temple.

"I don't have time to argue you silly looking sonofabitch! What kind of item is it?"

The people in the hall shouted at him indicating it was the Major's record fish in the glass case. Charles, who had come up from the marquee, was studying the late entry sheets and shouted across,

"General, it's the last of the Major's things! Everything else of his has been sold!"

"Give me that!" shouted the General as he tried to grab the microphone from the pulpit with his free hand.

"I will not!" yelled Shipley struggling to retain his precious microphone until the General dealt him a sharp left, knocking him out of his chair and all but off the stage and into the fireplace.

"Now hear this!" The General's voice boomed.

"This is General Chuck Verbeer! The Sheikh and I are bidding on the Major's stuffed salmon and we hereby bid the sum of twenty five thousand pounds!"

In the pub they were incredulous as the crowds roared.

"Plus commissions and whatever other costs there are so the Major ends up with the twenty five grand. Are there going to be any arguments?"

"No!" everyone shouted.

The General smacked Shipley's gavel down on the pulpit breaking its handle and yelled,

"Sold!"

Then he and the Sheikh rushed back to the office to the sound of thunderous applause.

"George, have you got your cheque book?"

"What? Yes, I think so, it's here somewhere," said the Major, digging into the inside pocket of his jacket.

"Well write that cheque now!"

"What?"

"C'mon George, we just bought the big fish for twenty five grand! Hurry man! You've only got..."

"Twenty eight seconds," said Bert Hughes, looking at his watch.

"Write George, for heaven's sake write!"

While the Sergeant counted down the seconds the Major did as he was ordered and wrote out the fastest cheque of his life to Rawlston for the twenty five thousand pounds and threw it on the table just as the count came to zero.

"You can't! I won't accept it! It's a fraud! A cheat!" screamed Rawlston.

"On the contrary," said the General, "the Major has just paid you the required twenty five thousand pounds for a new lease on his cottage and fishings in due time and in front of five witnesses. Six if we count your lawyer. So now he's legally entitled to stay in his cottage for another....how long, George?"

"Twenty five years, old boy," said a bewildered George Roberts.

"But you can't do this!" shouted Rawlston.

"Mr.Rolton! You told me that your condition was that I must buy the entire estate and so it is the entire estate I must buy! Now I find there is a cottage and some fishing you have rented out without informing me and this completely ruins my plans. The estate is no longer whole. I do not think I wish to purchase from you anymore!"

"What? But you said a million pounds! We agreed! I want my million pounds off you!"

Rawlston looked with hatred at the Major.

"This is all your fault you stupid old bastard!"

He suddenly threw himself across the desk intent on doing the Major serious harm, only to find the General's free hand gripping him by the throat.

"Sit down!" commanded Chuck Verbeer, pushing Rawlston back into his chair and training the revolver on him once more.

"This thing is far from over Rawlston. Right now you've got twenty five thousand pounds, no sale of your estate and you're facing a full military enquiry into your wartime activities."

"And I want to have an extremely serious talk to both you and Mr.Shipley about the recycling of goods through your auction business after you'd stolen them from the original vendors so that you could make huge profits for yourselves," said Bert Hughes. "Oh yes, our Mr.Rawlston here has been up to all kinds of tricks with his partner. I'm also sure the Inland Revenue will be extremely interested in talking to him and going back through his financial dealings over the years."

The General turned the screw.

"Sounds like a load of trouble for you Rawlston. Jail for about fifteen years should sort you out though, you'll be broke and an old man by the time you get out if you live that long. Proper justice for someone who has the blood of good men on his hands, don't you think?"

Chuck Verbeer had his man cornered and all Rawlston could do was sit there desperately trying to think of a way out.

"Of course if we were to adjust the price for the estate I might still be interested in purchasing," said the Sheikh

"Adjust the price?" asked Rawlston.

"Yes, it would seem in the light of the information we now know about you that you most probably are wishing to leave this place. I am taking into account that you were not truthful with me about the Major's cottage and fishing and I now make you an offer of this amount."

Taking up his pen the Sheikh smartly crossed the last zero off the figure of a million pounds that was on the contract.

"Wait a minute! That's only a hundred thousand pounds! Come off it! The estate's worth a lot more than that and you know it!"

"But are you, Mr.Rolton? Are you?"

"You bloody sheet wearing, lamb eating, pig ignorant..."

But the Sheikh had raised the pen again and Rawlston could not risk having another zero disappear.

"If I were you Rawlston I'd take the money and run, that is if you can get past the law," said the General.

Behind him Bert Hughes raised an eyebrow.

Rawlston's eyes darted around the room looking at each of them in turn and then at the contract. His brain raced as he sought to save his million pounds and himself, but the more he thought the more he realised that he was well and truly caught between a rock and an extremely hard place and that he only had one way out. After an interminable length of time he slowly reached forward and signed the contract.

"Here is the one hundred thousand pounds in cash, Mr.Rolton."

The one who was not the Religious One took a large amount of money from the suitcase next to the Sheikh and placed it on the table.

"Now I give you but one hour to leave my house for I do not wish to see you ever again. One hour! That is all!"

The General and Bert Hughes stood aside as Rawlston and his lawyer picked up the money and gathered their things in silence. As Rawlston passed him the General said,

"Wherever you run to Rawlston from now on and for the rest of your life my people will be watching you."

Bert Hughes closed the door behind them.

"But you have let him off lightly, General. In my country he would have had his hands or his head cut off. At the very least he would have been staked out in the desert for the carrion to eat."

The Religious One gave the Sheikh a derisory look at this exaggeration.

"Sheikh can you imagine the time, trouble and money it would cost to prosecute that guy? Yes it could be done, but I really like the fact that he's lost the biggest part of everything he gained from his illegal acts and now that he's been uncovered he's going to find life real tough, believe me. By the way, if I might say so, that was some pretty quick business thinking on your part, but I guess you people are used to haggling over prices."

"Ah, yes indeed," the Sheikh's dark eyes glistened with mischief, "but of course you will understand that normally we do it over camels."

As they smiled at the thought Bert Hughes was fiddling with his watch. "Funny thing, seems to be running a bit slow."

The Crow that was a Rook carefully positioned the nest so that most of it was hanging delicately out from the hole he had made in the hedge and then took off, climbed and circled the field.

'Well this is it then, time for a Rook to show the whole world! Time to prove to one and all the superiority of Rook brain and flying power! Now if I can just get this right all my problems will be solved!"

He power dived down on the hedge and came shooting along it aiming straight for the nest. His intention was to pick it up in his beak and trust that his speed would be enough to enable him to lift it into the air. A seemingly sensible and reasonable plan even if somewhat bold, but unfortunately his execution of it went ever so slightly awry.

He came onto the nest perfectly and at just the right speed, but instead of being able to pick it up as he wanted his momentum drove his head straight through the middle of it. Saddled with the entire nest around his neck he furiously beat his wings in desperation as he struggled to remain airborne. Out of control he careered from side to side as the nest, now adorning his neck like some grotesque scarf, swung him this way and that.

"Bloody Hell Fire! Bloody Hell Fire! What have I done? I can hardly fly! I'm not going to make it!"

However, looking like either a Crow or a Rook that had rammed its head through the centre of a large ring doughnut he was somehow beginning to defy the laws of gravity and ever so slowly climb into the air. As he struggled and strained against his cumbersome burden and began the perilous journey back to his home everything was against him. His strength was giving out and, even if he somehow did manage to gain enough altitude, how on earth could he ever hope to land on a chimney pot with this ungainly thing stuck around his neck?

He realised there would be only one chance were he to be so lucky as to make it back for if, as his speed slackened for landing, he did not immediately deposit himself and his load directly inside the chimney pot he would assuredly fall to his death.

"I don't want to die! I don't want to die falling out of the sky! It's the worst way for a Rook to go!"

Trapped by his nest collar it came down to his having just the one chance because he had only enough strength left to be able to make one run in to deposit himself and his load in exactly the right place. There was no hope of his going around to try again. This certainly was the time to prove to one and all the superior flying, and for that matter carrying ability of a Rook. As he began to cross the square he lined himself up on the distant chimney pot like some Lancaster bomber on a Dambusters raid and prepared to make his one and only most final run.

"Death or Glory! Death or Glory!" he cried as he repeatedly adjusted to the dreadful swinging weight of his nest necklace. Battling through the air currents he allowed for drift and carefully aimed at the rapidly approaching chimney pot.

"Steady! Steady! Left! Left! Up a bit! Whoops! Right a bit! Hold it! Hold it!"

Until the last split second it looked as if he was surely doomed, but in defiance of the great odds stacked against him the Crow that was a Rook managed to execute this most difficult and death defying of all aeronautical deeds to absolute perfection.

"Here you are darling!" he shouted as he closed in on the final yard of his dangerous journey. His wife looked up just in time to see her husband, saddled with his enormous cargo, enter the chimney pot and land right on top of her.

"What on earth do you think you're doing you stupid bird?" she screamed at him.

But before he could answer there came an ominously loud cracking sound from directly beneath them. She looked daggers at him. He looked back at her, their faces just inches apart. He was now wedged in the chimney pot with his head still jammed through the nest, completely unable to move. She was about to have a real go at him when there came an even louder cracking noise from beneath them and suddenly their entire nest, now weighed down by the new one he had so triumphantly brought her, engaged free fall and both it and they plummeted straight down the chimney into the waiting eons of soot below.

As Rawlston and his lawyer began making their way slowly out through the crowded hall Herpes, who had been lying seemingly out for the count under the feet of his impeccably turned out master, began to stir. His head lifted, his body vibrated as if he were throwing some kind of a fit and he suddenly and noisily expelled all of the obnoxious gasses that had been building up within his system. It was such an extremely loud occurrence that everyone for rows around turned and looked directly at Bob, who seemed not only unconcerned but completely oblivious to the sound of his dog's natural bodily function.

However being oblivious to it was one thing but avoiding the result of it was quite another for this had been Herpes' all time greatest performance, the one that would immortalise him into local legend forever.

Shipley, disturbed by this loud and rude noise, harrumphed and carried on.

Moans began emanating from those in the immediate vicinity of Bob as 'Fragrance de Herpes' wafted about, relentlessly expanding its range. The moans became louder, even though people were holding handkerchiefs over their faces to try and somehow stem the awful smell. They looked at each other in desperation through watering eyes, searching for some relief, of which there was none to be found as they were packed in so tightly for this last day that none of them could move.

Shipley began to stutter and stumble over the bidding as one by one the bidders seemed to collapse in front of him, either doubling up or covering their faces with items of clothing as they tried desperately to block out the stench. As the obnoxious gasses filtered throughout the hall murmurs of disgust developed into cries of desperation. The saleroom was degenerating into a sea of red faced, writhing, asphyxiating people all crying out for the windows to be opened.

Those standing at the sides, the last ones to be hit by Herpes' canine chemical warfare attack, finally turned to open the windows, but it was all going to be far, far too late to save any of them, for even as they were in the very act of doing so the village hall suffered a disaster of biblical proportions as the fireplace exploded.

A huge atomic cloud of jet black soot erupted across the middle of the hall, instantly obliterating most of the people present who all screamed as one as the mushrooming black cloud enveloped them. Out of the epicentre of this billowing black menace hurtled two screeching black projectiles from hell.

The two bedraggled Crows, one a Rook which had now burst free from its raffia collar on its free fall chimney descent and both aerodynamically impaired by their thick, heavy covering of soot, flapped and flopped their black tracer trail around the room, depositing even more soot upon the hysterical mob.

Tracking low across those seated, landing on the heads of screaming women and glancing off the walls they ricocheted around the hall, desperately searching for a way out.

Crows!

The blackened Herpes had unfortunately spotted the feathered intruders and stormed into the attack. This was more like it! No more boring lying down for him! Snarling and barking, jumping on and off and over people he added to the pandemonium as he went after the birds. His mad dog antics made the already desperate state of confusion in the hall considerably worse. In the limited visibility people who were attempting to force their way out began falling over each other as they tried to avoid the insane attack dog as it was led on a merry chase round and round the hall.

Shipley was completely black from head to foot as were his helpers. Both he and his pulpit, the stage and the entire fireplace end of the hall looked as if it had disappeared into a big Black Hole. Not a single person had been spared. The gigantic, exploding mushroom cloud of soot had comprehensively covered everyone and everything, permeating every available space and re-decorating the interior of the hall in a colour as black as midnight.

At long last the windows were flung open and the crowds outside exclaimed at the sight of the huge gouts of blackness that streamed from them accompanied by the screams emanating from the bedlam going on inside. The hall looked as if it was on fire with black 'smoke' pouring out of the windows and the main door.

People began to pour out themselves including Rawlston and his lawyer covered from head to toe in thick, black soot. Out of the doorway of the village hall there came a staggering, lurching line of blackened, coughing, wailing beings as if straight from a House of Hammer horror movie. It was a fearsome sight. Those outside at first rushed to help and then recoiled as the blackness was passed onto them. No one could make out what could possibly have happened in the hall.

Finally, out of opposite windows on either side of the building and to almost no one's notice in the melee, there flew two black, screeching demons from hell making their escape to freedom at last.

The General, the Major, the Arabs and the policeman walked out of the office into the blackened shell of the hall and looked in astonishment at the scene of devastation before them as the last of the people exited the main door. The jet black figure of Shipley, still sitting at his pulpit with his two white eyes silhouetted by total blackness, pointed a shaky finger at the fireplace and croaked something.

"Well, well, well if it isn't Soot of Soot Hall," said the General.

Bert Hughes sniffed the air.

"What's that smell?"

"Smells a bit like gas to me," said the Major.

"But there's no gas supply in here Major, plenty of soot though. I think we'd all be better off outside. Mind yourselves as you come through, gents."

The Arabs held their robes tightly to them and carefully picked their way through the hall. As they walked together across the square the General was talking quietly with the Sheikh.

"About the Major and the cottage, Sheikh."

"It is a good thing he can stay there, is it not?"

"Yes, it's really excellent, but there is a problem, I don't think he has enough money to be able to afford the rent."

"Ah, but he can work for me and do something on my estate, no?"

"I was wondering whether you would put him in charge of the salmon fishing? He'd be the best man to run them for you."

"So be it," he turned to George Roberts.

"Major I would like you to do something for me."

"Oh yes, old boy? Anything you want, you just tell me what it is and I'll see that it gets done."

"Good, good. I want you to run my fishings in the future in the best way that you see fit. Would this be possible?"

"Run the fishings? All two miles?"

"Yes. Is it as much as two miles? I did not know. Well in recompense for doing this work I shall immediately dispense with your rent. Would this be agreeable?"

"Agreeable? Why yes, it most certainly would! But look, are you really sure about this, old boy?"

"Yes I am sure, the General recommends you so it is done, you have my word."

Bert Hughes had a problem.

"You know I can't let either Rawlston or Shipley go, don't you General?"

"I guessed not, if they've broken the law you have a job to do."

"Absolutely. I don't even need to think about all the people they've ripped off whilst running their scheme. They're common thieves and thieves must be dealt with under the law."

The Sheikh spotted Takada and his friend.

"Ah, my friends, good day to you both!"

They were now at the beer tanker and the General stiffened once again at the sight of the two Japanese, but he was surprised to see the Sheikh embrace them as if they were family members.

"Gentlemen, may I introduce my two great friends Mr.Hiroyuki Takada and his friend whose name even I am unable to pronounce."

Bert Hughes and the Major shook hands with the two Japanese, who bowed to them. Takada turned to the General and held out his hand. Chuck Verbeer paused as if deciding whether to shake it or not.

"General, these two gentlemen are most interesting and great experts in the field of Japanese swords. I count on them both as my very good friends as I do you," said the Sheikh, quickly perceiving there might be a possible problem.

Slowly the General took Takada's hand in his and as he did so the Japanese bowed to him.

"The war has been over for a very long time, General."

Chuck Verbeer had to admit how true a statement that was and so, casting aside his misgivings, he said,

"Yes, it has, a very long time."

"We are people who should always try to look to the future."

"Well that's sensible. There are too many bad memories in the past."

"Yes, for both of us. May I buy you a beer?"

"No, let me buy you one."

"But I insist."

"My friends do not concern yourselves for I am buying beer for everyone!"

The Sheikh turned to those serving at the beer tanker.

"Beer for everyone if you please good people!"

Gradually as the beer was consumed the General and Takada turned the conversation to the sheer folly of war, the fact that no one ever came out of it a true winner and that they would all be better off working together to build a better future.

"Perhaps one day you could assist us in finding out what happened to some of our boys who never came back from the war?" the General asked.

"Whatever you need investigated it would be my privilege to help."

"Great," said the General.

Shipley sat there dejectedly nursing the black eye the General had given him, although you couldn't tell which one it was under his covering of soot. He had attempted to clean himself, but still looked like an old time chimney sweep as he sought to try and make the best of the remainder of the sale. There were only two of his blackened helpers in the hall with him, still faithfully trying to man the telephones. The three of them were alone as not one of the thousands of people outside dared enter the hall. There were just over two hundred lots to go and Shipley was determined to try and sell them, especially as the largest proportion were his and Rawlston's late entries. He tried to put all the things that had happened from his mind as he cleaned his sale book to a state where he could read the descriptions of the lots again.

Gathering himself he blew a large cloud of soot from his pulpit and another from the microphone and opened his mouth to attempt to restart the auction only to find the PA system was not working. Nor would it work again before being dismantled that evening as someone had cut the wires that connected it to the village hall.

The Little Saddlington auction was finally over.

Aftermath

The black limousine swept into the square coming to a halt in front of the General and Hetty Joy as they talked with Charles and Nancy outside the village hall. The Sheikh was his usual infectious self and appeared extremely happy about the way everything had turned out.

"We are travelling to Japan now, General, and I am a little concerned for my estate while I am away."

"How do you mean, Sheikh?"

"Well the farmer will look after the horses when they arrive, but there is no one to look after the house and the rest of the estate. Can you perhaps recommend to me some trustworthy person who might take care of this?"

"As it happens I think I might be able to..."

"I see him, Papa!"

They turned at the boy's shout and looked to where the Sheikh's son was pointing. Above the hall a large, black bird was powering its way straight up into the sun. As they shielded their eyes the bird let out a raucous cry as it continued on its towering climb.

"I'm free! Free at last!" screamed the Rook that was indeed a Rook as his climb took him ever higher into the clear blue sky. Finally, upon reaching an immense height, he stopped his climb and let out another great cry.

"I'm free! Divorced! Do you hear me? I'm a Rook and I'm free!"

With that he closed his wings and dived straight at the group of people standing in the square. Like a bullet he came, pulling out of the dive as he passed the roof of the hall with the air hissing from the edges of his folded wings and making the people duck as he shot close over their heads and giving out another loud cry.

"Free! Do you hear me? Free!"

Within seconds he had blasted across the square and, using his speed to go into another climb, he executed a perfect barrel roll as he soared out across the green, gliding on fixed wings and setting course for the distant Rookery.

"What an extraordinary bird!" exclaimed the Sheikh.

"He is happy, Papa! He is happy because he is free!"

The Religious One and the Sheikh looked down at his son and then back at the Rook, now disappearing into the distance.

"My son likes freedom. For him all animals and birds must be free or he is not happy. It is Allah who has made him this way and I am proud that he has chosen to do so."

As they stood there talking more villagers gathered to say goodbye to the Sheikh. Sergeant Hughes shook his hand and said he looked forward to his return. After a while it was time to go. The Sheikh paused before he got into the limousine as if he wanted to say something to his new found friends. It seemed for a moment as if he did not really want to leave them, but then he got into the car and it moved off as the group waved him goodbye. Reaching the end of the square the vehicle turned and came back past them at speed with the Sheikh leaning from a rear window.

"Goodbye my friends!" he shouted as he waved to them, "May Allah watch over you and may all your camels have two humps!"

The limousine sped out of the square, swung out onto the main road and disappeared from sight.

The Laird of the Highlands and Julius Polperro met at the tiny village station.

"Ye're no taking the high road with me, are ye Cornishman?"

"No fear Scotsman, no it's the low road for me down into the deep South West of England."

"Just as well laddie, just as well."

They shook hands and Julius walked across the bridge and faced Willie and his two sons from the other platform.

"Now remember Scotsman, don't go wasting money you can't afford to lose!" he shouted across.

"Aye, and if you ever come to Scotland," shouted Willie as his train entered the station, "just remember to keep going right on through!"

They smiled at each other before the train came between them.

Bill Boyd and his missus were saying goodbye to Mickey and Mrs.Mickey and Bob and Herpes at the pub.

"Look Bill, we've got to come to some arrangement about what I owe you for all the work you've done for us."

Mickey was greatly concerned to keep everything right between them.

"You mean pay me?"

"Yes, of course."

"Pay me real money?"

Bill was grinning.

"Yeah, real money. Come on, stop messing about. Me and the wife have reckoned it all up and we think that if we were to pay you..."

"Sorry mate, got to go, it's been great meeting you all."

He and his missus began hugging them.

"We've had a real good time. You wouldn't believe it but we almost have as much fun as this at home, don't we doll?"

"But you can't leave and not let us pay you something. This is out of order. We'll probably never see you again."

Bill looked at the three of them as he patted Herpes.

"No worries mate, you'll see us again I'm sure."

The Lancashire Lads were waiting outside as, with Mickey and his wife still protesting that it wasn't right Bill's not accepting some payment, Bill and his missus piled into the car. Bert Hughes arrived just in time to see them off, wished them a safe journey and away they drove.

"Now then, I've got something for you lot that Mr.Boyd left me strict instructions not to give you until he'd gone," announced Bert producing a couple of envelopes. He gave one to Mickey and one to Bob and they went back into the bar to open them.

"Tickets? He's left us some sort of tickets, luv," said Mickey as he read what the tickets were for.

"Blimey! They're for a cruise to Australia!"

"Don't be mad! Let's see!"

His wife and Bert pored over the tickets and found that it was true. There was also a handwritten message indicating that unless they used them and went to Australia, Bill and his missus would never speak to them again. The tickets were a present, there was no question of payment. In their excitement they had forgotten about Bob.

"Well this should please you 'cos I've got one as well!"

Mrs.Mickey was crestfallen.

"'Erp! Do you fancy going on a cruise then?"

"Don't be silly, you can't take a dog on a cruise, thank heavens."

Mrs.Mickey was relieved that Bob was only joking.

"Mind you it does say on this 'ere ticket, 'With one canine to be quarantined before departure'."

"Oh, my God!" exclaimed Mrs.Mickey.

Rubicon & Shipley went bust.

Even before he'd had a chance to count his takings from the auction Shipley found that a huge pile of advertising and printing invoices, along with those for the PA system and the mobile toilets, mysteriously appeared on his desk and within a month he was broke.

Both he and Rawlston were arrested and successfully prosecuted for theft. At the trial the judge gave special praise to the efforts of Charles Montgomery and Sergeant Hughes for bringing them to book. They both spent two years in prison after which they disappeared and were never heard of again, not even so much as a whisper. Doubtless the General's people still keep a watchful eye on Rawlston though, wherever he is.

When Rubicon & Shipley went bust the village got its hall back. The villagers bought it from the liquidator in a flash, pooling together some of the money they'd collectively made over the period of the auction. The first order of business was to get the chimney properly swept and remove all the soot from inside the hall so they could bring it back to being the hub of village life once more. As the auction had proved itself such a good money spinner and such good fun it was decided they should hold it once a year and that the utmost should be done to encourage people to come to it from all over the world so that the village could make some very useful money to go against the upkeep of the hall.

Nowadays the auction is always a time of great festivity and Charles has made an excellent auctioneer. He makes sure that the animal pens don't collapse, nor the pulpit, the fireplace doesn't explode, people are only charged a fiver for their seats, the roof slates are fixed properly and there are never more people in the hall than the Firemaster allows. He puts more than one marquee on the village green now and people take stalls to sell their various wares from, turning the auction into a two week country fair that thousands of people come to.

The Sheikh bought Johnny Enright's fields and took on Charles and Nancy to run his estate on recommendation from the General. The two of them celebrated their luck at having such a wonderful house to live in and set about keeping both it and the estate up to par.

Then the racehorses arrived, delivered to the farmer and taking up residency in their brand new stables, followed by the trainers, jockeys, grooms, stable lads and finally the media.

They went around taking pictures of everything and asking countless questions about the Sheikh that nobody could truthfully answer because no one really knew who the Sheikh was, where he came from, what he owned or how much he was worth.

So the media made it up.

Charles and Nancy soon found that as the Sheikh's operation got under way they were virtually running a hotel at the manor and absolutely loved it. Both took up riding and are currently planning to get married. The Sheikh renamed the estate 'Freedom Valley' and his horses consistently win races. They do say he's got a couple of hot ones coming along. The villagers, of course, back them all the way.

Bill Boyd and his missus went North with the Lancashire Lads and heaven only knows what they bought from them. Myrtle got a phone call asking her to clear part of the local garage so they could put everything on display and Bill kept going on and on about something called a Lagonda.

Mickey and Mrs.Mickey and Bob and Herpes went to Australia.

They had a right old time with Bill and his missus by all accounts. Herpes' gas problem was cured by some Aborigines who fed him something weird which made the 'Erp sleep for three days and nights, since when he has hardly ever broken wind, much to everyone's relief. They're all back safe and sound, but Bob's threatening to go to America soon. He keeps muttering something about 'missing a bit of female company'. Where he would get the money from for such a trip no one quite knows, but he has a fairly reasonable income now that he's head river bailiff, so maybe that explains it.

Dirk and Terry are Bob's assistant bailiffs and very good one's they have made too. They're both married and have quietened down considerably, becoming almost respectable. It must be something to do with their wives, those two American MP ladies Dolores and Dip. Good for them both it's been now they're no longer allowed to get on the wrong side of the law. There are more salmon in the miles of river around Little Saddlington these days than ever before and it has become well known as an area to steer clear of if you fancy doing a bit of poaching.

And then there's the Major.

Epilogue

Major George Roberts' School of Fly Fishing has become so well known that people come to it from all over the world. His clients include a big percentage of Americans who all seem to be ex-military types, something to do with the General's LAOS organisation.

Sometimes the Major can have twenty people on his weekly course and is absolutely in his element with nothing giving him more satisfaction than teaching them how to fish the Railway Pool.

He no longer has those awful nightmares having gained a steady cure from a number of his clients who talk to him about the war and their own experiences, many of which were worse than his own. This change in perspective seems to have eased his burden and has been a therapy the General most probably knew was needed.

Before the Great Day had ended the General had made an impassioned plea over the PA system from the pub for all the Major's things that had been sold that day to be returned and luckily, after refunds were made to the people who had purchased them, they all were. He and the Major phone each other once every week without fail and the General is coming over for the next auction.

The Major, ever a man with a conscience, could not get that dreadful ex-services home out of his mind and eventually told the General about it. One week later the home was purchased, the residents were moved out into hotels under supervised nursing and shortly the whole place was flattened. The LAOS organisation paid for a brand new purpose built nursing home with the most modern facilities to be erected on the site and the lives of those who choose to spend their remaining years there have benefited enormously.

Mrs.Ferzakerley makes up the packed lunches for the Major's fishing school, organises the bookings and cleans his cottage. He's put on a little weight due to her good cooking and is back to his old cheerful self, just as the villagers used to know him and they all reckon he's been blessed with a new lease of life. He goes to the churchyard regularly to tend to his wife's grave, but now someone usually goes with him, just so he doesn't dwell on the past that bit too much.

As you can probably imagine the Major never complains that the Sheikh's horses sometimes disturb the fish when they go thundering by along the gallop that runs close beside the stretch of river that his school operates in, or that his clients all excitedly rush out of the water and up the riverbank to see them as they pass.

Under his tutelage both Dirk and Terry have each caught a salmon using a rod and reel and a fly for the first time. They've come to understand George Roberts' great skill and knowledge and they've taught him one or two poaching tricks to keep an eye open for.

Very close the three of them have become.

Last year the Major taught the Sheikh's young son to fish and he actually caught a salmon. A six pounder it was and he and the Major let it go because the little lad wouldn't keep it. It started a bit of a trend amongst the fishing school and now people only take a fish home if they want to get it cooked or smoked. They take a lot of pride in putting their first one back for conservation purposes.

The Major presented the great fish to the pub and there it stays, proudly displayed on the main wall and thousands of people get to see it over a year, some of whom come a long way especially.

Mickey won't let the Major pay for any drinks in consequence of this extra business and, although the Major would never abuse such an arrangement, it has been yet another financial assistance and very good reason for him to regularly visit the Flying Start and spend some time with his friends.

THE END

www.ingramcontent.com/pod-product-compliance
Lightning Source LLC
Chambersburg PA
CBHW070750120626
46557CB00002B/524